£4·95

GW00992851

Selected Writings
of
Edward S. Curtis

Excerpts from Volumes I-XX
of
The North American Indian

Edited and with an Introduction
by Barry Gifford

Creative Arts Book Company / Berkeley

Third Printing

The editor wishes to thank Don Ellis for his support and belief in the worth of the material which enabled this book to be published.

Special thanks to Al Reid and his associates at the New Western Front Gallery, Mill Valley, California, for their interest and generous loan of the original printed text and photographs.

Cover photo of Edward S. Curtis by Edward S. Curtis

Published by Creative Arts Book Company
833 Bancroft Way, Berkeley, CA 94710.

ISBN 0-916870-00-6
Library of Congress Card Catalog #76-7891

CONTENTS

Foreword by Theodore Roosevelt   i
Introduction by Barry Gifford   ii
In Memory of Mr. J. Pierpont Morgan   v
Alphabet Used in Recording Indian Terms   vi
A Note on the Text and A Note on the Typography   vii
Original Title Page of Volume One   ix

SECTION ONE: Mythology   1
Navaho: Legend of the Night Chant
Sinkiuse Salish: Beaver Steals Fire
Awaitlala Kwakiutl: Dance Obtained from the Wolves
Hawunkwut Tolowa: The Man Who Caught the Ocean Cougars
         Hair-Seal He Played
Maidu: The Girl Who Would Not Use the Menstrual Hut
Washo: Origin Myth
Chipewyan: Da-Tsaʰ-Thi, Beak Excrement [Raven] Head
Hopi: Clan Legends
Clallam Salish: The Origin of Seals
Selawik [Eskimo]: The Woman Who Became a Bear

SECTION TWO: Ceremonies   27
Navaho: The Night Chant
Arikara: The Sun Dance

SECTION THREE: Medicine and Medicine-Men   43
Apache: Dance of the Gods
The Oklahoma Indians: Peyote Experiences

SECTION FOUR: Religion   49
Teton Sioux: The Vision Cry
Hopi: Deities
Nambé Tewa: Snake Cult

SECTION FIVE: Historical Accounts   71
The Papago

SECTION SIX: Arts   85
Apsaroke (Crow)

SECTION SEVEN: Warfare   91
Nootka

SECTION EIGHT: Social Customs   103
Tiwa: Kivas and Societies

APPENDIX ONE: Biographical Sketches   111
Brulé: Little Dog
Assiniboin: Long Fox
Assiniboin: Mosquito-Hawk
Ogalala: Red Cloud

APPENDIX TWO: Note on the Indian Music   115
by Henry F. Gilbert

APPENDIX THREE: Vocabulary   121
Western Algonquian Comparative Vocabulary

APPENDIX FOUR: Tribal Summary   131
Incidents of the Nez Percé War

LIST OF ILLUSTRATIONS   143
Joseph—Nez Percé
Mescal Bakers—Apache
Fasting
Piegan War-Bonnet and Coup-stick
Little Dog—Brulé
A Piegan Play Tipi
Potter Building Her Kiln
The Grizzly-Bear—Piegan
Drilling Ivory, King Island
The Bow-Drill, King Island
Tonenili, Tobadzischini, Nayenezgani—Navaho
Arapaho Maiden
Return of Scouts—Cheyenne
Piegan Camp

FOREWORD

In Mr. Curtis we have both an artist and a trained observer, whose pictures are pictures, not merely photographs; whose work has far more than mere accuracy, because it is truthful. All serious students are to be congratulated because he is putting his work in permanent form; for our generation offers the last chance for doing what Mr. Curtis has done. The Indian as he has hitherto been is on the point of passing away. His life has been lived under conditions thru which our own race past so many ages ago that not a vestige of their memory remains. It would be a veritable calamity if a vivid and truthful record of these conditions were not kept. No one man alone could preserve such a record in complete form. Others have worked in the past, and are working in the present, to preserve parts of the record; but Mr. Curtis, because of the singular combination of qualities with which he has been blest, and because of his extraordinary success in making and using his opportunities, has been able to do what no other man ever has done; what, as far as we can see, no other man could do. He is an artist who works out of doors and not in the closet. He is a close observer, whose qualities of mind and body fit him to make his observations out in the field, surrounded by the wild life he commemorates. He has lived on intimate terms with many different tribes of the mountains and the plains. He knows them as they hunt, as they travel, as they go about their various avocations on the march and in the camp. He knows their medicine men and sorcerers, their chiefs and warriors, their young men and maidens. He has not only seen their vigorous outward existence, but has caught glimpses, such as few white men ever catch, into that strange spiritual and mental life of theirs; from whose innermost recesses all white men are forever barred. Mr. Curtis in publishing this book is rendering a real and great service; a service not only to our own people, but to the world of scholarship everywhere.

THEODORE ROOSEVELT

October 1st, 1906.

i

INTRODUCTION
by Barry Gifford

Edward Sheriff Curtis was born near Whitewater, Wisconsin in 1868. At 19 he moved with his family to Puget Sound, and it was there that his fascination with both photography and Indians began. He constructed his own camera and in 1896 began his investigation of Indians living on the Seattle waterfront. His early portrait of Princess Angeline, the daughter of Chief Seattle, became one of his most famous photographs.

An experienced mountain-climber, Curtis, on one of his ascents of Mt. Ranier, rescued a near-frozen party that included Dr. C. Hart Merriam, Chief of the U.S. Biological Survey; Gifford Pinchot, Chief of the U.S. Forestry Dept.; and George Bird Grinell, the editor of *Forest & Stream* magazine. They later invited him to be one of two official photographers on a major expedition to the Bering Sea. Accompanying them on the expedition were naturalist John Muir, and ornithologist John Burroughs. It was on this trip, exploring Alaskan waters, that Curtis took his first brilliant series of Indian pictures.

His interest in Indians deepened, and Grinnell soon afterwards had Curtis spend a season with him among the Piegan and Blackfoot tribes in northern Montana. Curtis soon came to realize that he was witnessing the passing of a great race, and determined to preserve, through his photographs and ethnological notes, the customs and legends of the North American Indian.

He began his project in 1897, and in 1904 staged his first photographic exhibit in Seattle. Curtis financed the work himself for the first nine years, but in 1905 he met President Theodore Roosevelt at an exhibit of Indian pictures in Washington, D.C. Roosevelt was so impressed by the photographs (he later wrote the foreword to Volume One of the series) that he arranged for Curtis to meet with financier J. P. Morgan in New York, to see if he could be of any help. Curtis did so, and, after an initial rebuff, Morgan agreed to assist Curtis' project. By the time Curtis had completed his work, Morgan, and the Morgan estate, had contributed more than half of the total cost of $1,500,000.00.

Curtis decided to concentrate his study on the tribes west of the Mississippi, from New Mexico to Alaska, beginning in the southwest with the Apache, Jicarilla, and Navaho.

ii

He attempted to participate as closely as possible in the daily and ceremonial life of the various tribes, succeeding, in 1922, in becoming a Snake Priest in the Hopi Snake Cult ceremony. Professor Edward S. Meany, in his article "Hunting Indians with a Camera" (*World's Work,* March 1908), quoted one Indian elder as saying of Curtis, "He is just like us, he knows about the Great Mystery."

Curtis' reports on the individual tribes are invaluable. Though not as professionally detailed or complete as the research of academic investigators such as the California anthropologists A.L. Kroeber or Robert Lowie, Curtis chose what he felt were the most interesting aspects of each tribe. He and his assistants, most notably W.E. Myers, whom Curtis acknowledged in all but two of the twenty volumes, amassed information on all areas of Indian life, legend and lore: social and religious customs, mythology, cermonies, history, medicine and medicine men, folk-tales, primitive foods, warfare, the arts. Appendices to the volumes include biographical sketches, tribal summaries, songs, and comparative vocabularies.

It was assistant Myers who had the finest ear for phonetics, and who helped Curtis record over 10,000 songs, more than 700 of which are still intact in the University of Indiana archives. According to T.C. McLuhan, many biographical sketches were drawn first-hand: Bull Chief, for example, was able to trace Crow history through ten chiefs.

Curtis' scholarship involved extensive fieldwork: he studied the Little Big Horn battlefield with three Crow scouts who guided Custer's command, and interviewed Sioux participants who contributed still vivid recollections of the confrontation.

The project, originally estimated by Curtis to take fifteen years, took thirty, during which time he studied over eighty tribes and took 40,000 photographs. The twenty volumes, edited by Frederick Webb-Hodge, are each about 300 pages long, and contain in toto 1500 photogravure prints. Each volume is accompanied by a corresponding portfolio consisting of 36 or more copperplate photogravures, totalling 722 plates.

Curtis also produced a motion picture, "In the Land of the Head Hunters", in 1914, a native love story of the Pacific north coast, cast entirely with members of the Kwakiutl tribe. It showed briefly in Seattle, where, despite its sensationalist title (Curtis had hoped to raise money for further research with it), it was met with less than popular or critical acclaim. It has recently been restored, re-edited, and re-titled ("In the Land of the War Canoes") by anthropologists at the University of Washington.

He staged an Indian opera at Carnegie Hall on November 16, 1911, a running narrative accompanying films and music to depict the "vanishing race". Curtis compiled two books of Indian legends and folklore: *Indian Days of the Long Ago* and *In the Land of the Head Hunters,* published in 1914 and 1915 respectively, both of which until very recently were long out of print.

Curtis' insatiable drive to catalogue the North American Indian was a necessary one—by 1930, the final year of the project, there were few visible traces of the people that were once the sole occupants of a continent. The change in a hundred years was complete—no civilization had ever been removed and replaced so totally in so short a time. Curtis had been compelled to record the last vestiges of that passing, had in fact dedicated his life to it.

The 500 twenty volume sets of *The North American Indian,* of which only 272 were bound, are ensconced in rare book rooms of libraries and in the homes of private collectors. The cost of one of the Moroccan-bound sets, the publication W.H. Holmes, Chief of the Bureau of American Ethnology, said "should last a thousand years," is estimated to be in the tens of thousands of dollars. The New York *Herald* proclaimed the work as being "the most gigantic undertaking in the making of books since the King James edition of the Bible."

When Edward Curtis died on October 21, 1952, in Los Angeles, at the age of 84, he was generally unknown, and practically penniless. The publication of a *Selected Writings* allows the general reader a glimpse into the past, provided by a "shadow-catcher", as the Indians described the photographer, and should finally accord Edward Curtis the recognition he deserved during his lifetime.

IN MEMORY OF MR. J. PIERPONT MORGAN

In the final hour of producing this volume we are saddened and borne down with the loss of the patron who made the work in its full scope possible. To one who thought in detail the magnitude of the undertaking would have prevented coöperation. In this as in all matters with which he was associated he saw the scope; in a measure the magnitude. The fact that he was so able to comprehend this meant the rendering of a service to the world of art and literature of much value. It meant a substantial and comprehensive addition to the documentary knowledge possessed by the human race. The purchase of a picture or a book already produced is but a change of ownership. To make possible the production of an important picture or book is an actual addition to the sum of human knowledge and a forward step in the development of the race. In that thought lies the importance of Mr. Morgan's aid to this cause.

The American Indian possesses many unusual qualities and affords Science the opportunity of studying primitive life in one of its most interesting and important phases. Mr. Morgan made possible this study, which means a noteworthy addition to the records of the Indian race and one which otherwise would not likely have been possible. It is true the undertaking has required the coöperation of many others, yet the confidence manifested by Mr. Morgan at the outset resulted in that subsequent support which has aided so greatly in bringing the work to a stage that makes its completion assured.

Those who have joined us in furthering this national undertaking must feel like the members of a great family bonded by the desire of creative accomplishment, and as such a family we mourn the loss of the one whose philosophy made our purpose possible. While we are saddened by this loss we cannot let it weaken our purpose or retard our progress. Rather than that we must let his achievement be our inspiration toward the completion of the work in a larger and stronger way than even he in his unequaled comprehension dreamed of. The effort from now until the final volume is written will be for work so strong that there will be an ever-increasing regret that he could not have remained with us until that day when the last chapter is finished.

EDWARD S. CURTIS

April 16, 1913

ALPHABET USED IN RECORDING INDIAN TERMS

[The consonants are as in English, except when otherwise noted]

a	as in father	ḳ	a non-aspirated k
ă	as in cat	k̇	velar k
â	as in awl	q	as kw
ai	as in aisle	ṇ	as ng in sing
e	as in they	ⁿ	nasal, as in French dans
ĕ	as in net	r	formed with the tip of the tongue
i	as in machine	ħl	the surd of l
ĭ	as in sit	p̣	a non-aspirated p
o	as in old	ṭ	a non-aspirated t
ô	as in how	th	as in thin
oi	as in oil	śh	as in shall
u	as in ruin	'	a glottal pause
ŭ	as in nut	!	stresses enunciation of the preceding con-
ụ	as in push		sonant
ħ	as ch in German Bach	superior letters are voiceless, almost inaudible
g͟h	the sonant of ħ		

vi

A NOTE ON THE TEXT

The selection of writings has been based on the entire twenty volumes of *The North American Indian*. I have excerpted what I feel is most representative, as well as most interesting, from each of Curtis' headings. By its very nature any selection is subjective, but there is literally nothing in Curtis' life-work I find uninteresting. The ideal solution, of course, would be to reprint the entire twenty volumes, but until that is done it is hoped that this selected writings will serve as the authoritative available text.

B.G.

A NOTE ON THE TYPOGRAPHY

With the exception of the Note on the Indian Music by Henry F. Gilbert, which was typeset on an A/M Comp/Set 500, the typography of the original text has been preserved throughout. Selections made from appendices and sub-sections were printed in a reduced type-face, thus the recurrent discrepancies.

THE
NORTH AMERICAN
INDIAN

BEING A SERIES OF VOLUMES PICTURING
AND DESCRIBING

THE INDIANS OF THE UNITED STATES
AND ALASKA

WRITTEN, ILLUSTRATED, AND
PUBLISHED BY
EDWARD S. CURTIS

EDITED BY
FREDERICK WEBB HODGE

FOREWORD BY
THEODORE ROOSEVELT

FIELD RESEARCH CONDUCTED UNDER THE
PATRONAGE OF
J. PIERPONT MORGAN

IN TWENTY VOLUMES
THIS, THE FIRST VOLUME, PUBLISHED IN THE YEAR
NINETEEN HUNDRED AND SEVEN

SECTION ONE: Mythology

Navaho: Legend of the Night Chant
Sinkiuse Salish: Beaver Steals Fire
Awaitlala Kwakiutl: Dance Obtained from the Wolves
Hawunkwut Tolowa: The Man Who Caught the
    Ocean Cougars
    Hair-Seal He Played
Maidu: The Girl Who Would Not Use the
    Menstrual Hut
Washo: Origin Myth
Chipewyan: Da-T͡sa^h-T͡hi, Beak Excrement
    [Raven] Head
Hopi: Clan Legends
Clallam Salish: The Origin of Seals
Selawik [Eskimo]: The Woman Who Became
    a Bear

1

LEGEND OF THE NIGHT CHANT

Long years ago three brothers — the eldest rich, the second
a wayward, roving gambler, and the youngest a mere boy — lived
together among their kind, the Dĭnế people. Their only sister
was married, living apart with her husband. The gambler often
took property belonging to his brothers, going to distant corners
of the land to stake it on games of chance. On returning, he
never failed to relate a story of wonders he had seen — the Holy
People whom he had met, and who revealed many things to him.
His brothers never believed him, calling him Bĭlh Ahatĭnĭ, The
Dreamer.

One day they wished to go hunting, but did not want The
Dreamer to accompany them, so, going to the home of their
brother-in-law, they told him of their purpose, and all three stole
away. As the sun began its descent on the fourth day, it occurred
to Bĭlh Ahatĭnĭ that he had been tricked, so he started in search
of the hunters, hoping to meet them returning, that he might
help them carry their game and be rewarded with a pelt or two.
He travelled far, but had not come upon them when the sun
passed behind the distant hills. Near by was a deep, rock-
walled cañon, from the depths of which many mingled voices
could be heard. Bĭlh Ahatĭnĭ walked to its edge and peered over.
Back and forth from side to side flew countless crows, passing in
and out of dark holes in opposite walls. From below, when
darkness had shrouded all, Bĭlh Ahatĭnĭ heard a human voice
call in loud echoing tones, "They say, they say, they say, they
say!"

From the far side came the answer: "Yes, yes! What's the
matter now? What's the matter now?"

"Two people were killed to-day," continued the voice just
below.

"Who were they? Who were they?"

To which the first voice answered, "Anahailĭhĭ, killed at
sunrise, and Igákĭzhĭ, killed at dusk, by the People of the Earth.
They went in search of meat, and the hunters shot arrows into
them. We are sorry, but they were told to be careful and did

not heed. It is too late to help them now; let us go on with the chant."

It had grown very dark, and Bĭlh Ahatĭnĭ became greatly frightened, but he stayed to listen and watch. Muffled strains of songs came from the deep recesses in each cañon wall, — the gods were singing — and just within the openings, discernible in the glow of a fire, could be seen many dancers performing in unison as they kept time with rattles. Throughout the night firelight flickered from wall to wall and singing and dancing continued. At daylight the participants departed in all directions, so Bĭlh Ahatĭnĭ resumed the quest of the hunters.

He had travelled but a short time when he came upon his brothers, resting their heavy game packs on their journey homeward.

"Here comes The Dreamer," spoke his elder brother. "I will wager he has something marvellous to relate."

Bĭlh Ahatĭnĭ was greeted first by his brother-in-law. "You must have slept near here last night, for you are too far out to have made this distance since daylight."

"I did," he replied, "near a cañon that is surely holy. A lot of people had gathered to dance, the gods sang, and —"

"There, I told you he would have some lie to tell," interrupted the eldest brother, and started on.

"Go ahead," urged the brother-in-law; "tell us the rest."

"It's no use; no one cares to listen to me," said Bĭlh Ahatĭnĭ.

His younger brother, also incredulous, took up his burden and plodded off, whereat Bĭlh Ahatĭnĭ related all that he had seen and heard.

"You men must have killed those people they spoke about," he accused.

"No, it was none of us," his brother-in-law protested; "we have killed no people. Yesterday morning one shot a crow, and last night we killed a magpie, but there was no harm in that."

"I fear there was; they were hunters like yourselves, in search of meat for the Holy People, for the time disguised as birds," Bïlh Ahatíní ventured. Then, dividing the pack, the two hurried on to overtake the others.

" Well," asked the youngest, "did you hear a fine story?"

" It is not a lie," his brother-in-law retorted; "we killed a crow and a magpie yesterday, and the Holy People talked about it in the cañon last night. Look! There come four mountain sheep! Hurry, Bïlh Ahatíní, and head them off!" They had come upon the cañon where the strange voices had been heard. Four sheep, among large bowlders near the rim, were carefully threading their way out of it. The three dropped back, while Bïlh Ahatíní ran ahead and concealed himself near the ascending trail. As the sheep approached he drew his bow and aimed for the leader's heart, but his fingers could not loose their grip upon the arrow, and the sheep passed by unharmed. Bïlh Ahatíní scrambled up over the rim of the cañon and ran to get ahead of them again, but the bowstring would not leave his fingers as they passed. A third effort, and a fourth, to kill the game brought the same result. Bïlh Ahatíní cursed himself and the sheep, but ceased suddenly, for whom should he see but four gods, Yébïchai, appear before him, who had transformed themselves into sheep! Haschélti, in the lead, ran up to him and dropped his *balíl* — a rectangular, four-piece, folding wand — over him, as he sat, and uttered a peculiar cry. Behind him came Zahadolzhá, Haschëbaád, and Gánaskïdï; all were masked.

"Whence came you?" Bïlh Ahatíní asked them.

" From Kïnnínïkai," Haschélti answered.

"Whither are you going?"

" To Tségyïï, to hold another *hatál* four days from now. You had better come along."

" No, I could n't travel so far in four days."

But after a little parleying Bïlh Ahatíní assented. He was told to disrobe, and doing so Gánaskïdï breathed upon him, and his raiment became the same as that of the gods. Then all took four steps eastward, changing into mountain sheep, and bounded away along the cañon's rim.

The hunters in hiding became restless as The Dreamer did

not return, so ventured out where they could view the trail on which he was last seen. No one was in sight. One went to the rock where Bïlh Ahatíní first hid near the sheep and followed his tracks from hiding place to hiding place until the fourth one was reached, and there he found his brother's old clothes with his bow and arrows upon them. There he traced four human footsteps to the east that merged into the trail of five mountain sheep. The eldest brother cried in his remorse, for he saw that his brother was holy, and he had always treated him with scorn.

The gods and Bïlh Ahatíní, transformed to mountain sheep, travelled very far during their four days' journey, coming on the fourth day to a large hogán. Inside were numerous Holy People, both gods and men. When Bïlh Ahatíní entered with his four holy companions, a complaint at once arose from those inside against an earthly odor, whereat Haschélti had their charge taken out and washed with yucca-root suds.

Inside the hogán stood four large jewel posts upon which the gods hung their masks. The eastern post was of white shell, the southern of turquoise, the western of abalone, and the northern of jet. Two jewel pipes lay beside a god sitting on the western side of the hogán. These he filled with tobacco and lighted, passing one each to his right and his left. All assembled smoked, the last to receive the pipes being two large Owls sitting one on each side of the entrance way at the east. They drew in deep draughts of smoke and puffed them out violently. While the smoking continued, people came in from all directions. At midnight lightning flashed, followed by heavy thunder and rain, which Tónenïlï, Water Sprinkler, sent in anger because he had not been apprised of the dance before it was time to begin it; but a smoke with the assembled Holy People appeased him. Soon after the chant began and continued until morning.

Some of the gods had beautiful paintings on deerskins, resembling those now made with colored sands. These they unfolded upon the floor of the hogán during the successive days of the *hatál*.

The last day of the dance was very largely attended, people coming from all holy quarters. Bïlh Ahatíní through it all paid close attention to the songs, prayers, paintings, and dance movements, and the forms of the various sacred paraphernalia, and when the *hatál* was over he had learned the rite of Kléjĕ Hatál. The gods permitted him to return to his people long enough to perform it over his younger brother and teach him how to conduct it for people afflicted with sickness or evil. This he did, consuming nine days in its performance, after which he again joined the gods at Tsĕgyiï, where he now lives. His younger brother taught the ceremony to his earthly brothers, the Navaho, who yet conduct it under the name of Kléjĕ Hatál, Night Chant, or Yébïchai Hatál, The Chant of Paternal Gods.

BEAVER STEALS FIRE

A long time ago the sole inhabitants of the earth were the animals, who then were people, and the only fire was in a world above the sky. The animals assembled to discuss the question of how to obtain this fire, and it was decided that the leader of the expedition should be he whose war-song was the best. Muskrat sang first, but his song was not good. Others sang in their turn. A short distance away stood a little knoll, whence they heard the sound of some one whistling, and when they all hurried over they found there Coyote and his companion, Wren, who had a thick bundle of little arrows. Coyote was invited down to the council-place, and when he there began to sing his war-song it was found so good that the others immediately began to dance. He was at once given the task of obtaining the fire.

The next question was how to get into the upper world. Wren said he would shoot an arrow up into the sky, then another after it, and so on until there was a line of arrows reaching from the earth to the world above. When he had done this he, being the lightest, climbed up, taking with him a rope of bark. He at length reached the land above and let down the rope, to strengthen the string of arrows, and the others all started to mount. The last one was Bear, a greedy fellow, who took two baskets of food, which were so heavy that when he was half-way up, the rope broke and Bear tumbled back to the earth.

In the upper world it was found that Curlew was the keeper of the fire and the guardian of the fish-weir. Seeking to find in which house he lived, they sent Frog and Bullsnake to the village. These two crept over, and near the village stopped to listen. Frog was in the lead, and Bullsnake, becoming hungry, began to lick Frog's feet, and finally swallowed him with a gulp. He then returned to his companions, and when asked where Frog was would make no reply other than that Frog had been eaten. But he told where the fire was, and Coyote sent Beaver to steal it. The latter said that he would go to the river and float down on the water, pretending he was dead, and Curlew, watching the fish-weir, would drag him out and take him home for the sake of his soft fur. Then Eagle was to come, and, alighting on the house of Curlew, act as if he were wounded and unable to fly away, when Curlew's family would run out to capture him, and Beaver would thus be left alone in the house with the fire.

This plan was carried out, and Beaver started back for the river, carrying the fire; but just as he reached the water the people saw him and started in pursuit. He dived, and Spider was sent ahead by Curlew to spread his net in the river and thus catch Beaver, but the latter had already gone by, carrying the fire under his claws. Thrice more Spider attempted to set his net ahead of Beaver, but each time he was too late. So Beaver reached the rope and climbed down, and the others quickly followed. When those above saw that the others had fire, they ordered Frog to let the rain fall and put it out. It rained for a moon, but the fire was given to Prairie-chicken, who sat over it and kept it burning.

DANCE OBTAINED FROM THE WOLVES

Tlaqagílakŭmi ["copper-maker chief"] at Oqiówas on Hánwati ["has humpback salmon" — a small stream emptying into Knight inlet at Grave point] had four sons. One morning they still slept, and he became angry and shouted: "Get up, all of you, and go to wash yourselves! Are we going to our work or not?" Without replying, they went out into the water. One after another they rubbed tallow on their faces, turned the upper part of the paint-bag inside out, and dusted the red powder on their faces. Then the eldest said to his father, "Now let us go." They released the dogs and went upstream to the mountain Ќwaés ["sitter"], and climbed upward.

Suddenly Tlaqagílakŭmi exclaimed, "What is that, áate [lords]? We have never before seen that. To me it does not look like a stone."

The brothers took the dogs by the ears and made them look up, and the animals began to growl. They threw off the leashes, and the dogs dashed forward and began to leap about the object, barking loudly. Then the hunters came up and found it to be a large goat with one horn in the middle of its forehead. It had been dead for some time. While the young men skinned it and cut off the tallow, Tlaqagílakŭmi urged them: "Lords, hurry! There is something up there that looks dangerous. Clouds are beginning to hang on the summit!"

Soon they took up their loads and descended the mountain as rapidly as possible, but before they passed a bench on the mountain the snow began to fall in great flakes. When they were half-way down the old man slipped off a precipice and fell down the mountain, and was killed. The four brothers continued their descent, but soon the eldest slipped and fell down the mountain, carrying his dog with him. The other three went on, and the second brother fell to his death. Just before they reached the foot, the third fell and was killed, but his dog escaped. The two dogs now broke the trail for the youngest brother, and he succeeded in reaching a house and dragging himself inside the door. The dogs sat panting on the other side oɪ the doorway, but soon they began to dig in the fireplace, and from time to time one of them would jump into the hole as if to measure it. When his head barely rose above the level of the floor, he went to the young man and nosed him. "I suppose they wish me to go into that hole," said he to himself. So he sat down in it, and the dogs covered him with earth. Then he grew warmer.

When the fourth day passed without the return of the hunters, the brother of Tlaqagílakŭmi called the people into his house, and preparations were made to conduct a search. Wáĥet and Tláĥwŭnala made *héĥŭlofßísŭla* ["knitted on the feet"] out of goat-skin thongs, and went in advance. Behind them were men with four roof-boards, pushing one ahead of the others and so making a continuous road over the snow. By and by Wáĥet found a trail made by the dogs in walking to and from the house, and he and his companion soon were peering in through cracks in the walls. Buried in the warm earth and ashes of the fireplace up to his neck, the young man perceived that there were people outside, and with his last breath he cried, "*Ya!*"

"*Ya, áte!*" they responded, and ran in; but he was dead. Then they returned to the main party, who, when they heard that the youth was dead, declared: "We will stop here and make a fire. You go and bring the body."

So the two dug the body out, wrapped it and placed it in a large basket, and thus carried it to the canoe. Now, when they returned to the village there was another council, and the advice of the wisest man was this: "The best thing is not to break down our chief's house [on account of the supposed death of the young man]. We will place this body in the bed, then we will leave this village and go downstream to the mouth. We will make a little house for this chief's wife, so that she may sit in it and look through the doorway at the body."

All this was done. For four days the woman kept going down to the river to bathe, some days four times and some days thrice. On the third night she heard something walking about outside her hut, and on the fourth evening just at dusk a wolf howled on the opposite river-bank. When it ceased, another answered on her side of the stream. Then another howled below her, and a fourth above her. The wolves were inviting all the animals to sing and dance in the house where the dead man lay.

The woman felt that something good was coming. Though she kept her eyes on the body, the wolves, unknown to her, had taken it away. Still she thought she saw it in the house. It began to grow dark, and dimly she saw people, many of them, going into the house, and a voice in one of the corners of the room said, "Put the fire under!" From another corner came another voice, "Let our fire blaze up!" In the third corner another voice spoke, "Burn, fire!" A fire blazed up, and a fourth voice spoke from the other corner, "All you people of different tribes, make ready!" The first speaker resumed, "Now take hold of your batons!" From the second speaker came the words, "Let the holders of the batons stand up!" The third commanded, "Now beat time rapidly!"

Then came the sound of heavy beating, and the house seemed to shake with the dançing. The woman could see the standing baton master shake his baton and then suddenly give a sweep of the arm, and the beating ceased. After this had been done four times, all the people in the house cried out, "*Yihi...!*" Small whistles sounded, and the chief of the wolves entered, a big white animal. On his back she saw her husband, alive, clasping the wolf's neck with his arms. She seemed to see his dead body lying on the bed, yet there he was alive on the wolf's back. After four songs the wolf men began to dance.

The woman could not remain quiet. She moved toward the house, but at the same time the fire began to die, and the speaker cried: "*We, we, we, we!* Go and see! Some common man is near the house."

"Send no one but me!" cried Mouse. He went out to the woman and she whispered, "Whatever you are, I *tlúgwala* you!"

Said Mouse, "Come no closer." She gave him a bracelet to keep her secret, and he returned to the house and reported, "I have been round the world, and there is no one here."

The fire blazed up again, and the beating was resumed, and the woman crept closer again, eager to see what was being done. Again the fire sank, and again Mouse was sent, and the woman paid him with an abalone-shell ear-ring.

The sky was now beginning to change color, and in order to end the dance they beat four times without singing. At the end the first speaker said, "We have done enough!" The second repeated, "Yes, we have done." The third spoke: "Put away our batons!" The fourth finished: "Put our dance masks in a secret place!"

The woman could not see what became of the hundred wolves: they were gone, and the house was empty and the fireplace cold. The young man, her husband, was in the bed where the body had been placed. She returned to her hut and said to herself: "Oh, I do not know what I am going to do with myself! But there is no use trying to hurry things."

When the sun rose the woman walked out of her hut and sat a short distance from the house. After a long time she moved a little closer, and next she sat outside the door of the house. Then she sat on the step inside the door. She was watching the bed, uncertain whether her husband was really dead. Now he moved slightly, just enough to show her that he was alive. She made no movement, but sat watching intently. He raised his head, and soon sat upright and spoke: "Come in a little farther." She sat on the right side of the room, and he asked, "Was it long ago that you came?" But she only looked without replying, for she wished him to speak four times and thus assure her that he was actually alive. Then he asked, "Did you come as soon as they started? Did you see all that was done?" Still she said nothing, but nodded her head. "Did you keep in your mind everything that was done?"

And now she answered, "Yes, I know it all."

"Did you note everything and keep in your mind what was said?" "Yes, all."

"Go to that first corner and try to repeat what was said there."

The woman did so, and then likewise in the other corners. "It is true that you heard everything from the very beginning," said her husband. "There are two slaves belonging to your father, and two belonging to my father. We will use them, placing one in each corner, and you will instruct them. Go to your father's house and we will show them how to imitate these things, and after they have learned it we will call all the tribes. Tell your father to burn spruce branches in the house for four days, and to clean it out so that it will smell good."

After carrying this message to her father, the woman returned and accompanied her husband up the river to the hut where he had been buried in the fireplace. There he left her and went alone up the mountain. The snow was gone, and soon he found the third brother and sprinkled on the body the living water which the wolves had given him. The young man rubbed his eyes, sat up, and said, "I have been sleeping a long time!" Thus also the other three were saved, and all came down the mountain together.

Now the wives of these three brothers had remarried, and because this woman had remained true and had been strong-hearted to go to the mountain with her husband, they regarded her highly, and as they walked they surrounded her as if to protect her from danger. When they reached the place where the young man had been lying dead, they all went in and the woman showed them the secret things that had been done there. Then they crossed the river to the new village, and just at dusk came into the house of her father. A great pile of fuel was there, ready to be kindled.

So the ceremony was begun just as the wolves had done, and after the fourth beating of the batons came the great white wolf with the young man on his back. At the same time there were suddenly present around the fire a hundred wolves — not real animals, but wolf-skins stuffed with hemlock twigs and animated by the power of the wolves.

After the tribe had thus been instructed, it was decided to show the new dance to all the tribes. The people therefore embarked and went to Taíaquḥl, while Tlaqagílakŭmi and his four sons went on foot to the shore opposite Taíaquḥl. Beside them walked the image of the great wolf, carrying on his back all the paraphernalia of the dance: the batons, the masks, and the *sísiutl* sounding board. The people, expecting them, had arranged four catamarans of four canoes each, and now crossed to them. There did not seem to be much, yet when everything was loaded into the canoes they were filled. On the return voyage the wind rose and two catamarans were wrecked, and all the masks, the batons, and the *sísiutl* were lost. The wrecks drifted out of the inlet, and Káwaṭilikálla of the Tsawatenok found them and thus obtained this dance of the wolves. The brothers then made masks and batons and a wooden *sísiutl* in imitation of those that had been lost, and they gave the first performance of *wálas-áḣaaq*.

THE MAN WHO CAUGHT THE OCEAN COUGARS [1]

A man was looking for good luck. He would run along the beach from Taghéstlɓa to Tátat-ṭŭn, and whenever a breaker came rolling in he would leap under it. He would run from one village to the other and back again twice in one night. When he became cold, he would go into the sweat-house and warm himself.

One night he saw something near the line of breakers. He thought it was two pups. He caught them and took them home. He hollowed out a block of wood, filled it with water, and placed them in it.

In the morning he went to look at his pets. They were *tĕt-tí*ⁿ*chhu* ["in-ocean monster" — ocean cougar]. They grew rapidly, and each time he went to look at them they seemed to be hungry and ready to spring at him. The fifth night they leaped out and pursued him, but he was a swift runner and they could not catch him. He knew that these animals feared elk-horn, and he made a club of horn. The next night when they pursued him, he turned and tapped them with the club, and they stopped. He made a fence around the bowl of water, so that they could not get out. They became fond of him.

He heard that a man at Ḥwéstŭnnǎ-tŭn [a Tututni village at Whalehead, in Oregon, north of Natltanḗ-tŭn] had two animals like his pets, except that they were land animals and he heard that the man would set them on any person who passed. They were devouring the people. He decided to take his pets to that place and have a contest. He led them to the place and left them in the brush, saying: "I will go first. You remain here and watch. I will shout when they come after me."

Then the owner of the cougars saw him coming. He said to his pets, "Get ready!" He let them go. Then the man shouted to his ocean cougars, and they came bounding out of the brush and killed the mountain cougars. The people of that place began to shout disapproval, but the ocean cougars leaped upon them and killed them. Then they turned against their master, and he had to kill them with his elk-horn club.

HAIR-SEAL HE PLAYED [2]

Five nights he was going about in the darkness. His father slept in the sweat-house. His father asked, "Do you hear anything when you are going about?"

"No, I never hear anything," he said. "I never see anything."

"You will never get riches," said his father. "There is no use in your going about at night looking for good luck. You might as well sleep."

But he had heard his father say to other youths: "Up on that mountain yonder is a great bird. He is the one that is rich." This bird was never seen except when dead hair-seals came ashore. The youth covered himself with a seal-skin and lay on the beach like a dead seal. He put his head under a bunch of kelp.

Birds of every kind that eat carrion flocked about him in the morning. Last of all he saw two great birds coming from afar. They alighted on the beach and walked about looking at the man, cocking their heads this way and that. They wanted to see his eyes, for they always ate the eyes first. He had his hands ready to grasp them. One of them came close, and he caught it. It flapped its wings, and almost lifted him from the sand. But he had heard his father tell others what to do. He tied some of his hair about the bird's neck. He said, "I give my hair for your riches." The bird then flew away. He watched it fly to the top of Winchuck mountain and perch in a tree. When night came, it was still in the tree.

That night the youth had a dream, in which the bird said: "Go up to that mountain, and under the tree where you saw me sitting, look for money. You will find shell money in abundance. Do not show it to everybody. Put it into a large basket and do not look at it until ten days have passed." This he did, and at the end of ten days he found a large basket full of shell money.

---

[1] Narrated by Joe Hostler, Ḥawŭnḳwŭt Tolowa.

[2] Narrated by Joe Hostler, Ḥawŭnḳwŭt Tolowa. The title of the myth is Srísrĕnĕs Tŭ́ghŭtlaiⁿ ("hair-seal he-played"). The story is of the North Coast type. If it were included in a collection of Kwakiutl tales nobody would question its right to be there, were it not for the reference to the custom of sweating.

THE GIRL WHO WOULD NOT USE THE MENSTRUAL HUT

There was a girl who was having her first menses. Instead of going into the grass hut, she went into the mountains with her husband. She told him to climb a digger-pine and throw down some cones. He climbed up and threw down a cone. He said, "Try it; see if they are ripe."

She struck it with a stone and hurt her finger. She looked at it, and struck again, and again the stone struck her finger. She looked long at the finger.

The man in the tree was watching. He asked, "How is it?" He was wondering what she would do with the blood.

She answered, "It is all right." She licked off the blood. Again she struck her finger, and again licked off the blood. She kept licking at her blood, and then began to eat her flesh, singing, "*Dámiyâta pêâ mísin* ['I-am-crazy eating myself']!" She devoured her whole body up to the chest. The man was still in the tree.

She said, "Come down, let us go home." But he feared to come down. He left his voice in the tree, and leaped down on the other side upon a rock, and ran away. The girl was rolling about on the ground. She hurled herself against the tree, and there was a crash like thunder. The tree shook, but the man did not fall down. Again and again she did this. Then she called out, "Come down!"

The voice in the tree answered, "I am coming."

At length she said, "He must be deceiving me." She went around the tree and saw where he had leaped upon the rock, and followed him, rolling along the ground. She would strike the rocks with the crash of thunder. Then she overtook the man and struck him. He was thrown high into the air, and when he fell he lay there a mere head with arms and chest. They went into the sky and became the thunder.

When mosquitoes get their stomachs full of blood, they take it to her, but they do not tell that they obtain it from people, lest she strike and kill people for their blood. They tell her it comes from oaks, so she strikes trees in hope of finding blood in them.

ORIGIN MYTH

Tulíshi [wolf] was the chief of those who first inhabited the earth. When they decided that it would be best if they became animals of various kinds and made way for a new race of human beings, Tulíshi placed in a water-basket a quantity of cattail-down and seeds, and some grass. He set it aside and told the others to watch it. So they stood in a circle and watched it. A moon passed, and there was the sound of voices in the basket. They were indistinct. Tulíshi poured the contents on the ground. There were people of three kinds. In the centre he placed the Wáshiu [Washo]; on the west the Ṭĕubímmŭs [Miwok] and the Ṭánniu [Maidu]; and on the east the Páliu [Paviotso]. When the newly created people were seen, Kĕwĕ [coyote] protested that they ought to have four fingers like himself. But Lizard stood up on a rock and said, "No, it is right that they have five fingers like me." Kĕwĕ insisted: "They cannot do anything with five fingers. When I want to kill anything, I bite it." But Lizard declared that it would not look well for these new people to bite. They must use their hands, they must have five fingers. Kĕwĕ cried: "Do not make me angry! I will burn you!" But Lizard took refuge under a rock.

Then Kĕwĕ secured the assistance of Mouse and went with him to the east. There were those who had pine-nuts. He sent Mouse into the house where the cones were lying. Mouse carried them out, and Kĕwĕ ran away with them clinging to various parts of his body. He brought them home and asked, "What shall we do with these?"

Tulíshi said: "These will be for the Wáshiu and the Páliu to eat. Plant them and they will become trees." So they planted the nuts, which grew into trees, and Tulíshi told Mátus [measuring-worm] to mark off plots of ground for each family.

Kĕwĕ changed the original people into various kinds of animals. A great warrior became jack-rabbit, and his eagle-feathers became long ears. One who carried an ember wherever he went, to light the campfire, became sagehen, and the black spot of the sagehen's breast is a mark made by the ember.

DA-TSÁᴺ-ṮHI, BEAK EXCREMENT [RAVEN] HEAD [1]

DAṮSÁᴺṮHI, whose mother was a captive Cree, was a great leader in the border country between the Cree and the Chipewyan along the line from Athabasca lake to Cree and Caribou [Reindeer] lakes. He sometimes associated with the Cree, sometimes with the Chipewyan, but mostly with the latter. Fighting was a mania with him. All feared him, but none could kill him. He was called Raven Head because of a skirt of raven-skins, the beaks of which were tied together, two and two.

The people were camped beside a lake, and Raven Head went for birch-bark to make a canoe. While he was absent, the Cree attacked the camp, and when he and a small boy who had accompanied him returned, they found everybody dead, even the old grandmother with whom he lived. He said, "I am going to sleep here." He placed the dead in a heap and said to the boy: "While I sleep, if you see the Cree coming, call to me, 'Wolverene is coming!'" He slept so long that the corpses were rotting beside him. His power was working to bring the Cree back. At last the boy saw a large number of canoes approaching, and he called, "Wolverene is coming!" But Raven Head lay there like a dead man. He called again, and Raven Head leaped up. When he saw the Cree, he sent the boy into the bush. The Cree did not recognize him, for he was creeping about, crying, calling upon father and mother, as if he were a small boy. The Cree said one to another, "There is a boy we did not kill." They came ashore and leaped out of their canoes. But Raven Head turned suddenly and with a large bone broke their legs and arms. He made them sit in a circle and called for the boy. He gave him his spear and let him kill all the crippled Cree.

---

[1] Raven Head (not Crow Head, as the name is usually translated) was probably, like Little Shaky-leg, a historical person, a long-ago hero of the Chipewyan.

CLAN LEGENDS

MIGRATIONS OF THE RATTLESNAKE CLAN

When all the race of human beings emerged from the lower world at Sipapuni,[1] the tribes scattered, each going in the direction it chose. The Cougars and Doves proceeded northward along the east side of the cañon, and on a high mesa at Tokonabi [2] they built a village of stone houses, and called it Tokóna.

One day the son of the Cougar chief stood looking down at the rushing river, and he began to wonder whither all this water went. With such a volume constantly flowing into it, a place should soon become full, and overflow. He decided to find that place and ascertain why it did not overflow. When he mentioned the plan to his father, the chief said, "My son, you cannot go."

"Yes, but I must find whither this water goes."

"When, then, will you start?"

"I shall start in four days," said the youth. "Now I am going to devise something in which to travel. I want my sisters to prepare food for my journey, and you must make pahos."

Then the youth descended to the stream and found a large cottonwood log, which he hollowed out with fire and provided with a round door for each end. His father summoned the head men and they prepared pahos, and on the fourth day the chief's son placed in the hollow log his food and his pahos, a gourd full of water, and a short, pointed stick which his father had given him with the advice that if the log became stranded he should prod its side in order to cause it to start on. While his sisters and the people wept, he entered the log, and from the inside he sealed the doors with piñon-gum. The men rolled it into the stream, and it drifted away and soon disappeared.

For many days the log was carried onward, but at last it stopped and failed to move when he prodded the side with his stick. Cautiously, little by little, he opened the door, and no water entered. He removed the door altogether, and found himself on the edge of a great expanse of water, where the waves had cast him up. Then he crept out, and said to himself: "I wonder where I shall go? It is my own fault that I am here alone. But I will do the best I can." He beheld a ladder projecting from the middle of the ocean, and he

---

[1] Located by the informant in the Grand cañon above El Tovar hotel.
[2] Somewhere above Lee's ferry.

said to himself, "I wonder if that is the place to which I am going?" He opened his bundle of pahos, selected the one that had been made for the person who lived in the ocean, and fastened it to his belt. He made a ball of meal and cast it toward the ladder. It rolled away over the water, straight to the ladder, down which it disappeared. Behind it the waters divided, and on this path the youth proceeded to the ladder, dry of foot. A voice invited him to descend, and in a moment he found himself in a kiva, in the presence of an old woman who merely remarked, "Have you come?"

"Yes," he answered.

"You arrived a long time ago," she said, "but you did not know it. I am Hûzûịn-wûhti ['shells woman']."

The youth gave her the paho, saying: "This is for you. My father made it for you."

"Thank you!" she said. "Nobody has made for me anything like this for a long time, and I am very glad to have it."

Soon the ladder began to shake, and a handsome man came down with many pahos and much cornmeal, all of which he gave to the woman, who sorted out the pahos, muttering to herself, "This is for good crops, and this is for rain, this for children, this for game." Some she angrily threw aside, because they had been planted for evil [that is, for sorcery].

Now the Sun spoke to the youth: "For a long time it has been your desire to come, and now you are here. You must look closely, and heed what I say. Your father has made these pahos for Nánanivo-monwitúyŭ ['world-regions chiefs']. It will be that there will be plentiful crops, and all will be well with your people. It is a long time you have been travelling, and the people are growing anxious. You must go home. I will take the rest of these pahos to those for whom your father made them, to those who live underground. You have seen what I brought. I have brought pahos for both good and evil, and you have seen the scalps I brought. There has been a fight this day, and I am always the first one in any battle: I get the first scalp, and after that the warriors may take scalps. People who ask for good, for long life, for good crops, and everything that is good, shall always ask in the morning, and people who ask for the bad shall always ask at any time of the day, at noon or at evening. These bad things I have sometimes granted."

Then the Sun descended through the floor of the kiva, and on the following morning Hûzûịn-wûhti told the youth that he would find his home by directing his course to a certain mountain in the north. So he returned to the shore over a path made by casting another ball of meal, and started northward, following the river.

Now when he arrived at the foot of the mountain in the north, he came upon many rattlesnakes lying everywhere. He stopped and inquired if they would harm him, and when they assured him they would not, he went on, picking his way among them. More and more numerous they became, and on the top of the mountain he was compelled to tread on many of them. At the very peak of the mountain he found a ladder, and descending it he beheld many people, relatives of the reptiles he had seen on the mountain. The chief said: "You are a man! You have entered our home. You are the only one who has ever done so."

"I do not know," he said. "I do not think I am a man. But you are men."

They gave him a smoke, and, having finished, he told them that Hûzûin-wûhti had sent him to ask their aid in getting home. But they said: "We are not the ones to grant this. We are only the guards. We guard our chief, who is below." So they allowed him to pass down another ladder, and there was Ísanavaiya, the Rattlesnake chief, sitting alone. He looked up and demanded: "How is it that you have come? How is it that my guards have admitted you? You must be a man!"

"No, I do not think I am a man. I have come a great distance, and I will have a hard time returning home. I do not know how to find food, and I come to you for help."

Then the chief taught him the Snake ceremony and the songs, and sent him up the ladder. In the upper room he found a girl prepared for the journey, and the two started northward, the Rattlesnake girl carrying food in a bundle on the top of her head. She never ate with the young man, and whenever his food gave out, she would remove her belt and shake her body, and food would fall down from it. For the Rattlesnake people had food under each overlapping scale of their bodies.

After years of travelling they reached Tokonabi, and in due time the girl gave birth to many little rattlesnakes, and, though they were reptiles, the people were fond of them. But when the rattlesnakes bit some of the children [1] the people became angry and departed southward, leaving the rattlesnakes behind.[2] At every camp, as they journeyed, they erected the Snake altar and sang for rain, and the rain always came. After a long time they arrived at the village Wûko-ki ["great house"], where the Lamáti dance was in progress, and here they met other wanderers, the Squash people and the Flute people, and the two bands united.

From Wúko-ki a runner Tsámaheya went eastward in search of people, who, it was rumored, had emerged from the earth in that quarter. He reached the mountains in the east, and, going to the top to look for signs of people, he found two little boys playing shinny. These were the war gods Pökán-hoya [" ———— little"] and Palóṇao-hoya ["echo little"]. In reply to their questions he said: "I am searching for people. But I am exhausted. Can you help me?" Although they assured him they were no better travellers than he, going always on foot and driving their shinny-balls before them, they said they would ask their brother, meaning Arrow, the Arrow feathered with feathers from the wings of a bluebird. They shot an arrow southward, and it travelled far onward to an inhabited place, and there thrust itself into the ground.

"Somebody has come!" shouted the people, and they gathered around. "I am searching for people," explained Arrow. "Our elder brother has been going about, but he has become exhausted and I am travelling for him."

The people said: "We have just come out from the underworld, and we are waiting for instructions from our chief." They sat in a circle about their chief, who was a Kachina. Then the chief uttered the cry of a Kachina and motioned with his head toward the north-west, and the people said, "By the gesture of our chief, we are going toward the place from which your elder brother has come." Then the Arrow took the message to Tsámaheya, who at once started homeward; but at Akúka-vi-túqi ["Acoma place moun-tain" — Mesa Encantada] he stopped, and lived with the people there.

When the people at Wúko-ki, after waiting long realized that Tsámaheya would not return, they sent Antelope to find him. By following his trail Antelope discovered him at Akúka-vi-túqi; but Tsámaheya declared that he would remain there, and said that when the people were holding the Snake ceremony they should beat on the floor and he, hearing the sound, would come to help them bring rain.

In company with the Flute and the Squash people, the clans from Tokonabi departed from Wúko-ki, and near Oraibi wash they divided, the Squash clan founding Múṇyá-ovi, near the present Oraibi, and Chukubi. The Flute clan went eastward and settled at Lengyaobi [about thirty miles northeast of Walpi], while the clans from Tokonabi continued their march eastward. Midway between East and Middle mesas they established a village.

One day footprints were discovered in the sand, and the chief, searching among the rocks that were piled up on that part of the mesa now occupied by the central houses of Walpi, found there a man, a tall, handsome man living alone. This was Másôŭ. He said he had long been wishing that people might come, and promised to visit their village on the following day. The next morning the people saw Másôŭ start from the foot of the mesa on the west side, masked, carrying a short club filled with all kinds of seeds. When he neared the village, he ran toward the people and threw his club over their heads, in order to frighten them, but they stood fast, unafraid; and the chief ran to him and embraced him. Then Másôŭ told of a vow he had made, that if they proved to be people of courage, they should have his land. "This will be the first and the last meeting between us," he said. "From this time on I shall be invisible. I go below, but I shall always live here." Then he left them and from that time he was invisible, except that very rarely he has been seen dimly at night.

Not long after this the people moved toward the mesa and built the village Kuchaptuvela on the northern side of the terrace below the present Walpi. Later they built Kisakobi on a slightly higher level, and after the destruction of the Spanish priests [in 1680] they founded Walpi on the very top of the mesa.

The Origin of Seals [1]

There was a Clallam chief who had a most beautiful daughter, and so proud of his rank was he that he could find no one worthy of her. Hence he was greatly angered when he noticed that she was about to become a mother. But the girl did not know what was the matter with her and swore that she was a maid. In the course of time a male child was born. Its grandmother wished to keep and rear the infant, but the old chief was too angry to listen to such a plan, and he had a cedar box made and the bottom covered with pitch. In it he placed the infant on its back, and the pitch held it fast. Then he set the chest adrift at the mercy of wind and tide.

In his novel craft the boy drifted until he grew to manhood. He struggled continually to free himself, and at last, when the hot sun warmed the pitch, he succeeded. Once ashore he set out to find supernatural power, and after a few days he obtained the power of keen-eyed Fish-hawk for hunting and fishing. He went on and received the power of Eagle, and then he came to the home of the Thunderbirds, whose daughter he married. Here he lived happily, every day donning the Thunderbird skin of his wife and thus pursuing whales with the others. His mother-in-law was the best whale hunter, but she never hunted unless the others failed to bring in game. She it was who warned the young man not to attempt the capture of the first whale he saw on any expedition, for it would prove to be not really a whale, but an enormous clam whose neck, floating on the water, resembled a whale. This clam was the enemy of the Thunderbirds, and many had tried to catch it, thinking it a whale, only to be dragged to the bottom of the ocean and devoured.

One day the young man, feeling that he had great power, determined to capture the monster, and he swooped down, buried his talons in the great neck, and struggled to fly aloft. He pulled the neck out so far that it looked like an enormous snake, and then it would irresistibly contract and threaten to drag him beneath the waves. At last the Thunderbirds from their mountain home saw the battle, and perceiving that the clam was nearly conquered, they all flew down and laid hold of the neck. But the great clam only pulled the harder, and almost dragged them all below. Then the young man called upon his guardian spirits, and with a terrific effort the clam was torn from the bottom and carried through the air to the home of the Thunderbirds.

Now the young man determined to punish his grandfather for the cold-blooded manner in which he had been set adrift. In the form of an eagle he flew over the village, and his grandfather and all the people ran out to shoot at the bird. The arrows seemed to strike and pierce the eagle, and the archers thought they would surely bring it down; but the eagle was holding the missiles together, end to end, until they reached nearly to the ground. Then swooping down in great circles as if badly hurt, the bird let the line of arrows come within the reach of his assailants. Expecting to pull him down, they laid hold of the arrows, but the eagle flew off over the water and dropped them into the sea, where they became the first seals.

---

[1] Related by a Clallam.

SELAWIK

THE WOMAN WHO BECAME A BEAR

Pïsíksolïk, a great hunter, lived alone with his wife and two children, none of whom had ever seen other people. Pïsíksolïk was such a killer of game that his caches and even the entranceway to his house were always filled with meat. He hunted only for large game, such as bear and caribou, which he slew as easily as ordinary people caught rabbits and ptarmigan.

One time, after killing a female bear and her two cubs with his two-pronged spear tipped with horn, Pïsíksolïk sickened and soon died, despite the careful nursing of his wife. She sorrowfully bore the body, wrapped in bear-skins, to a grave, and erected poles closely about it to keep wild animals away. On the grave mound she placed all the weapons of Pïsíksolïk. All through the summer season the woman wept bitterly and mourned long for her husband.

One day, when the cold was intense and the snow lay deep, a bird hopped to her door and sang:

Pïsíksolïk in the far country is married now.
Pïsíksolïk in the far country is married now.

The woman heard, and hurried to the grave. It was open; the body wrappings of bear-skins were thrown aside, and the weapons were gone. Foot-tracks began at the grave and disappeared in the distance.

The puzzled woman returned home, determined to search for her husband. First she soaked a bear-skin to make it pliable. Next she placed some skinning boards along her sides and breasts, and then, slipping into the skin, laced it tightly in front. Thus no arrow or spear could injure her. To try out her power as a bear, she went into the forest. She found that with the strength in her paws, the strength of a full-grown bear, she could easily smash down trees and uproot stumps. As she went through the woods, a wide trail was marked by the broken trees. The woman returned home, confident of her ability and strength, and determined to set out after her husband; but first she dressed her two children in skins of bear cubs, left them plenty of food and water, and enjoined them not to leave the house before she returned.

For many days the wife followed the trail of Pïsíksolïk and ultimately arrived at a large house where the tracks ended. Just then a young woman came out of the door and stopped, startled to see a bear so close. She ran inside and told her new husband, Pïsíksolïk, that a bear was by the entrance. Pïsíksolïk, as well and strong as ever, snatched up his weapons and ran out, but the Bear-woman chased him to the roof of a cache before he could string his bow. From there he shot arrows and hurled his spear at Bear-woman, his former wife. None of the missiles took effect, but glanced off. Bear-woman began to climb the cache. Pïsíksolïk, now greatly frightened, jumped down, ran for the nearest tree, and climbed it. Bear-woman, with one full stroke of her paw, toppled the tree to the ground. With the other paw she crushed the skull of Pïsíksolïk. Next she hugged and squeezed the young woman until she was lifeless, and dropped the body beside that of the man.

Bear-woman journeyed home, and, when arrived, found that she could not get out of the bear-skin. It had grown to her own flesh, and she was now a real bear. The woman then led her children, who had become bear cubs, down the valley, where they lived on berries and rodents. Once she thought of returning to the house, but it smelled so strongly of humans that the mother and cubs soon departed. From that time they were true bears and lived in the open.

SECTION TWO: Ceremonies

Navaho: The Night Chant
Arikara: The Sun Dance

CEREMONIES — THE NIGHT CHANT

A description of the ritual and form of the Yébĭchai ceremony, — Kléjĕ Hatál, or Night Chant, — covering its nine days of performance, will give a comprehensive idea of all Navaho nine-day ceremonies, which combine both religious and medical observances. The myth characters personated in this rite are termed Yébĭchai, Grandfather or Paternal Gods. Similar personations appear in other ceremonies, but they figure less prominently.

First Day: The ceremonial, or medicine, hogán is built some days in advance of the rite. The first day's ceremony is brief, with few participants. Well after dark the singer, assisted by two men, makes nine little splint hoops — *tsĭpaⁿsyázhĕ kĕdán* — entwined with slip-cords, and places them on the sacred meal in the meal basket. Following this, three men remove their everyday clothing, take Yébĭchai masks, and leave the hogán. These three masked figures are to represent the gods Haschĕ́ltĭ, Talking God, Haschĕbaád, Goddess, and Haschĕ́lapai, Gray God. When they have gone and passed to the rear of the hogán, the patient comes in, disrobes at the left of the centre, passes around the small fire burning near the entrance of the hogán, and takes his seat in the centre, immediately after which the singing begins. During the third song Haschĕ́ltĭ enters with his crosssticks — *Haschĕ́ltĭ balíl* — and opens and places them over the patient's body, forcing them down as far toward the ground as possible. The second time he places them not so far over the body; the third, not lower than the shoulders; the fourth time, over the head only, each time giving his peculiar call, *Wu-hu-hu-hu-u!* Then Haschĕ́ltĭ takes up a shell with medicine and with it touches the patient's feet, hands, chest, back, right shoulder, left shoulder, and top of head, — this being the prescribed ceremonial order, — uttering his cry at each placing of the medicine. He next places the shell of medicine to the patient's lips four times and goes out, after which Haschĕbaád comes in, takes one of the circle *kĕdán*, touches the patient's body in the same ceremonial order, and finally the lips, at the same time giving the slip-cord a quick pull. Next comes Haschělapai, who performs the same incantations with the *kĕdán*. Again Haschélti enters with the cross-sticks, repeating the former order, after which he gives the patient four swallows of medicine, — a potion different from that first given, — the medicine-man himself drinking what remains in the shell. This closes the ceremony of the first day. There will, perhaps, be considerable dancing outside the hogán, but that is merely practice for the public dance to be given on the ninth night. The singer and the patient sleep in the hogán each night until the nine days are passed, keeping the masks and medicine paraphernalia between them when they sleep.

Second Day: Just at sunrise the patient is given the first ceremonial sweat. This is probably given more as a spiritual purification than in anticipation of any physical benefit. To the east of the hogán a shallow hole is dug in the earth, in which are placed hot embers and ashes, — covered with brush and weeds, and sprinkled with water, — upon which the patient takes his place. He is then well covered with blankets. The medicine-man, assisted by Haschélti and Haschěbaád, places about the patient a row of feathered *kĕdán*, and then commences to sing while the patient squirms on the hot, steaming bed. After singing certain songs the medicine-man lifts the blanket a little and gives the patient a drink of medicine from a ceremonial basket. He is again covered, and the singing goes on for a like time. Later the blankets are removed and Haschélti and Haschěbaád perform over the patient, after which he goes to the hogán. The brush and weeds used for the bed are taken away and earth is scattered over the coals. This sweating, begun on the second day, is repeated each morning for four days: the first, as above noted, taking place east of the hogán, and the others respectively to the south, west, and north. The ceremonies of the second night are practically a repetition of those held the first night. During the third song Haschélti enters with the *Haschélti balíl*, placing it four times in the prescribed order and giving his call; then he goes out, re-enters, and takes from the medicine basket four sacred reed *kĕdán*. These he carries in ceremonial order to the four cardinal points: first east, then south, next west, lastly north. Next stick *kĕdán* are taken out of the basket, which holds twelve each of the four sacred colors. These also are carried to the four cardinal points — white, east; blue, south; yellow, west; black, north. After all the *kĕdán* are taken out, Haschḗltĭ again enters with the *Haschḗltĭ balíl*, using it in directional order and giving medicine as on the night before.

Third Day: It is understood that the patient has been sweated in the morning, as on the second day. On this night he is dressed in spruce boughs by the assisting medicine-man, bound around the wrists, arms, ankles, legs, and body, and fastened on the head in the form of a turban. After several songs, Nayĕnĕzgani and Tobadzĭschíni cut the boughs from the body, using a stone arrow-point as a knife. Then the boughs are cut into fragments over the patient's head, after which the singer takes a feather wand, points it toward the four cardinal points above the fire, and brushes the patient, chanting meanwhile. At the end of the brushing he points the wand out of the smoke-hole, at the same time blowing the dust from it out into the open air.

Fourth Day: The ceremonies this day do not begin until later than usual, probably nine o'clock. Haschḗltĭ and Haschĕbaád dress and go out. The patient disrobes and takes his place. The assisting medicine-man digs a small hole just between the patient's feet, and encircles it with a line of *tádĭtĭn*, or pollen, leaving an opening to the east, after which the patient dons a mask. Haschḗltĭ enters, followed by Haschĕbaád, who carries a small spruce tree. The former puts sacred pollen in the hole four times, each time giving his call; then Haschĕbaád plants the tree in the hole and fastens its top to the patient's mask; the mask is then pulled off the patient's head by his jerking quickly away from the tree. This is the first night in which the ceremonies are continued until dawn. After the unmasking, the singers take their place at one side of the back of the hogán and begin singing to the accompaniment of a basket drum. A youth and a maiden are required to sit in the hogán throughout the fourth night, the ritual requiring that these be persons who have not had sexual knowledge.

Fifth Day: This is the last day of the sweating, and the day on which the first dry-painting is made. Just at dark this painting, a small one, is begun inside. In size it would square about four feet, and is placed close to the back of the hogán. There are three figures in the painting: the central one being the patient, the one to the left Haschĕltĭ, the one to the right Haschĕbakŭ^n. Around this painting, at all sides except the eastern, feather wands, *ndiá*, are stuck in the ground; in this case twelve in number. Foot-tracks are made in the sand with white meal. Haschĕltĭ and Haschĕbakŭ^n dress ceremonially, mask, and go out, after which the patient enters and takes his position on the central figure of the dry-painting, facing the east. The effort this night is to frighten the patient and thus banish the evil spirits from his body. The two maskers come running in, uttering weird, unearthly howls, in which every spectator in the hogán joins, feigning great fear. The masked figures make four entries, each like the other. In many cases the patient either actually faints from fright or feigns to do so. The patient then leaves the dry-painting and it is destroyed. None of the sand or other pigments used in this painting is applied to the patient's body, as is done with that of later paintings. The next part of the fifth night's ceremony is the initiation of new members into the Yébĭchai order. No one who is not a member of the order is allowed to enter the ceremonial hogán. At the time of the initiation Haschĕltĭ and Haschĕbakŭ^n are outside in the darkness. The initiates enter and sit on the ground in a row — the males naked, the women dressed in their ordinary mode. They dare not look up, for should they see Haschĕltĭ before being initiated, they would become blind. One at a time these novices take their place in the centre of the hogán and the initiatory rite is performed over them.

Sixth Day: This is the first day of the large dry-paintings. The painting is commenced early in the morning, and is not finished until mid-afternoon. The one on this day is the whirling log representation. After it is finished, feathers are stuck in the ground around it, and sacred meal is scattered on parts by some of the assisting singers. Others scatter the meal promiscuously; one of the maskers uses a spruce twig and medicine shell, applying meal to every figure and object in the painting. Then the medicine-men all gather up portions of the sacred meal, putting it in their medicine pouches. The patient soon enters and takes his seat in the centre of the painting. The usual incantations are gone through, after which the colored sands of the painting are applied to the corresponding parts of the patient's body, then gathered up and carried off to the north. During the day two sets of beggars go out to the neighboring hogáns. These personate Haschělti, Tónenĭlĭ — Water Sprinkler, the God of Water, who is really a clown — and as many Haschěbaád as care to go out. The beggars carry whips made of yucca leaves, and one who does not respond to their appeals for gifts is whipped, — if he can be caught, — which creates a great deal of amusement. The personators act like a company of clowns, but at the same time they gather a large quantity of food. When the day is thoroughly taken up with dry-painting and ceremonies, there is less of the ceremonial at night. The medicine-men, to the accompaniment of the basket drum, sing for a short time only on this sixth night, while outside the late evening is spent in dancing by those who are later to participate in the closing dance.

Seventh Day: This day is practically consumed with the making of another large dry-painting. The masked men go out on another begging tour, also, and the medicine ceremonies and the destroying of the dry-painting are practically the same as those of the day before, while during the evening the medicine-men sing to the accompaniment of the drum.

Eighth Day: The dry-painting is finished about three o'clock in the afternoon. After its completion there is a large open-air initiation. To become a full member of the Yébĭchai order one must first be initiated in the hogán; the second initiation is a public one; the third, another inside the hogán; the fourth, another in the open. These different initiation ceremonies, the same in point of ritualism, may be carried over several years.

Ninth and Final Day: To the average person and to the Indians as a whole the last day is the Yébǐchai dance. From a distance the Indians have been gathering during the two previous days, and the hospitality of the patient's family, as well as that of all the people living in the neighboring hogáns, is taxed to the utmost. And from early morning until dark the whole plain is dotted with horsemen coming singly and in groups. Great crowds gather at the contests given half a mile from the hogán, where horse-races, foot-races, groups of gamblers, and throngs of Indians riding wildly from race-track to hogán fill the day with hilarity and incidents memorable to all. Toward the end of the day preparation is made for the closing part of the nine-day rite. Great quantities of fuel have been brought from the distant plateau, and placed in many small piles at each side of the smooth dance ground to the east of the hogán. As soon as it is dark the fuel is ignited, making two long lines of camp-fires, furnishing both light to see the dancers and warmth to the spectators, for the Yébǐchai cannot be held until the autumn frosts begin, when the nights have the sharp, keen air of the high altitudes.

With the gathering darkness the human tide flows toward the medicine hogán, illuminated in the dusk by the long lines of camp-fires. All gather about and close around the dance square, having to be kept back by those in charge. Men, women, and children sit on the ground near the fires. Many on horseback have ridden up, and form a veritable phalanx back of the sitting spectators. The dance does not begin at once, and those assembled spend the time telling stories, jesting, and gossiping. Belated arrivals make coffee, or do hurried cooking around the fires.

Some distance to the east of the dance ground is a brush enclosure where the dancers prepare for their part in the rite. There, too, is a fire for light and warmth. The men in preparation remove all clothing, save short kilts, and paint their bodies with a mixture of water and white clay. Anyone who may have experienced the enjoyment of a sponge bath out in the open on a cold, windy night can appreciate the pleasure of the dance preparation. The dancers are impersonators of Navaho myth characters, twelve usually taking part. No qualifications are necessary other than that the participant be conversant with the intricate ritual of the dance. The dance continues throughout the entire night, one group of men being followed by another. The first twelve men dance through four songs, retiring to the dressing enclosure for a very brief rest after each. Then they withdraw, and twelve others dance for a like period, and so on. The first group sometimes returns again later, and the different groups vie with one another in their efforts to give the most beautiful dance in harmony of movement and song, but there is no change in the step. The several sets have doubtless trained for weeks, and the most graceful take great pride in being pronounced the best dancers. The first group of grotesquely masked men is ready by nine or ten o'clock; they file into the dance enclosure led by Haschĕltĭ, their naked, clay-painted bodies glinting in the firelight. While wearing masks the performers never speak in words; they only sing or chant. To address one in conversation would incur the displeasure of the gods and invite disaster. Time is kept by the basket drum and the rhythm of the singing.

The white visitor will get his best impression of the dance from a short distance, and, if possible, a slight elevation. There he is in touch with the stillness of the night under the starry sky, and sees before him, in this little spot lighted out of the limitless desert, this strange ceremonial of supplication and thanksgiving, showing slight, if any, change from the same performance, held on perhaps the same spot by the ancestors of these people ages ago. As the night wears on the best group of dancers come out. They are, perhaps, from the Redrock country, or from some other far-away district, and have been practising for weeks, that they might excel in this dance. The most revered song of the Yébĭchai is the Bluebird song, which is sung at the approach of day, and is the closing act of the drama. With the last words, " *Dóla anyí, dóla anyí,*" the assembled multitude start for their homes, near and far, melting into the gray of the desert morn, and by the time the sun breaks above the horizon the spot which was alive with people a few hours before is wrapped in death-like stillness, not a soul being within range of the eye.

THE SUN DANCE

The Sun Dance [1] of the Arikara, in its two principal features —
the personal supplication for spiritual strength for the individual and
the tribe, and the forceful promulgation of precepts of virtue in
women — was strikingly like the ceremony among other tribes of the
plains, but in its details it differed considerably.

When a man decided to give this dance, he went among the people
of the village, asking for arrows. After collecting a number, he carried
them for purification to the priest of the ceremony; then filling a
pipe, he took it with the arrows to a man who had a very fast horse.
Tendering him the pipe, he said: "My friend, I wish you to help me;
I am going to make the Sun Dance and I wish you to take these arrows
and kill me a fat buffalo." The man smoked the pipe, signifying his
consent; then the herald called for men to join the hunt.

They assembled at once, and one of them took from the sheaf of
arrows one that seemed the best, which he coated with paint. This
arrow the owner of the fast horse was to take, and no other, for with
this he must kill the buffalo. When the party went forth and the
herd was sighted, he must first single out the animal that had been
described by the priest of the dance and kill it. Before any butcher-
ing could be done, the leader of the hunt, first instructed by the priest,
removed the skin from the face, head, and back of the slaughtered
animal in such manner that a broad strip down the length of the back
connected the tail and the skin of the head. This done, the others
butchered and piled the meat on four horses, and the skin was placed
on the fast horse, which was then led to the village, the others following. The priest and the dancers went to the edge of the village to
meet them, and three men who had decided to dance took the skin on
their shoulders, one at the head, one at the middle, and one at the tail,
and carried it about the village, stopping at various places while the
people made presents to the buffalo-skin, heaping them upon it.
These with the skin were carried into the medicine-lodge

Inside this structure the priest covered the hair of the skin with
white clay. Then he called four noted warriors, who after dark went
into the woods and selected a straight tree with a forked top. They

---

[1] Called *Akúchíʃhhwnáhu* ("house whistle"), in reference to the constant blowing of
eagle-bone whistles in the ceremonial lodge.

cleared away the brush around it and remained there keeping constant vigil. In the morning they returned toward the village, running zigzag after the manner of scouts, stepping stealthily as if they saw enemies. Their approach was heralded by shouts, and people gathered on the housetops. The men assembled at the edge of the village, and the priest with the three dancers — those who had borne the buffalo-skin about the village — went out to meet them. One man in the party stepped forth, dropped his blanket in a heap, and quickly retired, and one of the bravest warriors ran and kicked it, thus symbolizing the striking of an enemy. The priest approached the scouts and asked the news, and was told that they had sighted a large village, meaning of course the tree, which represented the enemy. While the three dancers advanced to meet the scouts, they cried and prayed for success in war, such as these four brave men had experienced. Meanwhile the families of the dancers prepared food for the scouts.

During the day twenty men were appointed, and sometimes one woman with them, to fetch the tree. In preparing to set forth, these men went about the village confiscating horses, as well as spears, shields, and other implements of war, for from the time they left the village they played the part of enemies of their people. At nightfall they went out to guard the tree in the same manner as the four scouts had done.

Early the following morning the people of the village, men and women, donned their best clothing and mounted their best horses, the men with their weapons. Under the leadership of the three dancers, who travelled afoot, they proceeded toward the tree and stopped some distance from it. The four scouts went forward and soon returned with the news that the enemy was at hand. The word was spread among the attacking party; every one, simulating great excitement, made a mad rush for the tree, while the twenty who had been its guard through the night rode out to intercept them. A mock battle ensued, lasting until the larger party reached the tree, where they halted. They surrounded it, and to a captive girl wearing a scalp tied to her hair was given an axe, which she used to notch the tree; then it was passed to a girl of the tribe, presumably virtuous, but who might have been suspected of being otherwise. If she accepted the implement, it became the duty of any man who of his own knowledge could challenge her, to do so, when she must drop the axe; should this happen, she was sure to die shortly, for she committed an act of sacrilege by accepting the position. It was believed also that a false accuser soon would die. If unchallenged, the girl cut the tree, and, as it fell, a shout of victory went up as though an enemy had been slain.

A length of about twenty feet having been trimmed and cut off, the three young men, whose period of fasting had begun with this morning, assisted by a fourth man, lifted the heavy green pole and bore it to the village, in the centre of which it was deposited. The young women remained in the woods to gather bundles of willows, which they tied to the saddles, and the men to cut poles for the framework of the shelter in which the dance was to be held. Just before sunset the three dancers entered a sweat-lodge, prepared by the priest, for a purifying sweat. The priest and a few others accompanied them, while one woman sat in the middle at the rear and another just beside the entrance. A third woman carried in the stones and closed the entrance. During the sweat the priest sang, and when the singing was finished the women prayed for the success of the men in war. At times one of the three dancers, wishing to be specially favored of the spirits, raised himself from the ground by grasping the framework of the lodge, thus exposing himself to the fiercest heat.

A bunch of choke-cherry sticks was tied in the crotch of the ceremonial pole to represent an eagle's nest, and from this was hung the buffalo-skin, head downward, so that the spirit of the buffalo might look down and impart its strength to the dancers. As the pole was raised to be placed in the hole already prepared for it, one of the three dancers with an eagle-bone whistle in his mouth ran up its length to the nest and back again, moving his arms in imitation of an eagle's flight. The falling of the pole into the pit was greeted with a shout, as if a victory had been won. The women of the village then built the dance-shelter, with its entrance to the east, and at the opposite side was erected a low booth of ground-cedar for the priest and the singers.

The priest and his helpers, old men whom he had chosen to paint the young dancers, one of them for each dancer, dressed in deerskins wrapped about the waist. The singers for each day were from a different society. Before the singing began a girl was given a rattle, which she held up toward the men in the audience as a challenge. If anyone could personally dispute her claim to purity, it was his duty to do so, and if she were justly accused she relinquished the rattle and sat down disgraced. If her chastity were not impugned, the maiden continued to wield the rattle, and the singing began with great rejoicing. The priest and his assistants danced in a circle, blowing constantly on their eagle-bone whistles and adding much to the furor and excitement. As they danced, any woman who so wished arose, and holding a bunch of willow in her hand, danced, challenging all men to question her honor. The three dancers, with any others who wished to join them, began dancing, and continued, with intervals of rest, throughout this night, and if their strength sufficed, until the close of the third night following, the singers changing frequently. On the morning of the third day, such participants as wished to do so went to different places on the prairie, where each individual was pierced through the muscles of his back by an old man previously engaged by him for that purpose. Skewers were inserted, and to them were tied with thongs a number of buffalo-skins. The sacrificer, moaning and crying out, then dragged the skins into the dance-lodge, around the village, and back to the starting point, where his sponsor withdrew the skewers.

About noon of the fourth day the priest went out of the booth and stood opposite the pole. Such dancers as remained steeled themselves for their final effort of endurance. Joining hands as the priest waved his buffalo-tail fan about his head as a signal, they ran around the pole, each until he fainted from sheer exhaustion. A helper placed cedar leaves on burning coals, and the priest waved his fan over the unconscious men until they revived. As each one regained consciousness he dragged himself to the burning cedar, exposed his body to the smoke, then crawled back to his place. When the last one had been revived they described their visions. Each dancer during the ceremony had promised the supernatural powers some portion of his body; he now informed the old man which part he had offered, and it was cut off in further sacrifice to these mysterious powers.

SECTION THREE: Medicine and
Medicine-men

Apache: Dance of the Gods
The Oklahoma Indians: Peyote Experiences

DANCE OF THE GODS

The Gáŭn Bagúdzĭtash, or Dance of the Gods, is the one
ceremony of the Apache that bears any material resemblance to the
many Yébĭchai dances or "chants" of the Navaho, and even then
the only feature common to the two is that the men, typifying
gods, wear elaborate masks. The Apache are not unfamiliar
with the making and employment of dry-paintings for the treat-
ment of the sick, as has been seen. Originally the dry-paintings
and the *gáŭn*, or gods, always appeared together, but in recent
years the Gáŭn dance has been conducted preliminary to and as a
part of medicine, puberty, and war ceremonies. Captain Bourke,
in his "Medicine-men of the Apache" (Ninth Report of the
Bureau of Ethnology, 1892), speaks of this as the Spirit or Ghost
dance. Though performed infrequently now, as compared with
other dances, on account of the expense and of disapproval by the
agents, the Gáŭn Bagúdzĭtash is unquestionably the most popular
ceremony conducted by the Apache.

Four always, but generally five, deities are impersonated in
this dance — Gaŭnchĭně of the east, Gáŭncho of the south, Gáŭn
of the west, Gaŭnchí of the north, and Gaŭněskídě the fun-maker.
These are arrayed in short kilts, moccasins, and high stick hats
supported upon tightly fitting deerskin masks that cover the
entire head. Each carries two flat sticks about two feet in length,
painted with zigzag lines representing lightning.

For the dance a circular plot of ground, fifty or sixty feet in
diameter, is cleared of stones and brush, and four small cedar
trees are planted about its edge, one at each of the cardinal points.
All in attendance assemble in a circle outside the trees, leaving an
opening at the eastern side. Unheralded the five masked personators march in from the east and take position in front of the
cedar trees, the fifth man standing behind the fourth at the northern side. Four drummers with small drums and an indefinite
number of drummers around a large one, at a signal from the
medicine-man in charge, who sings, begin drumming. The personated gods dance all about the circle, making motions with
their sticks as if picking up and throwing something away,

followed by blowing with the breath for the purpose of expelling evil spirits from their midst. While this is going on the fifth masker, Gaŭnĕskídĕ, performs antics designed to amuse the audience. When the songs are finished the dancers depart in an eastwardly direction, whence they came, and all rest.

The drummers begin the next period in the dance by beating their tomtoms. As soon as they commence the *gáŭn* again appear, coming from the east as before, and stop in single file in front of the cedar tree on the eastern side. There the spectators throw *hádíntĭn* upon them and offer prayers, after which the five *gáŭn* take the same positions as before in front of the small trees. Upon the trees little wheels of cedar twigs have been hung; these the dancers now take, and each dances toward the fire in the centre of the circle and back four times. As the gods dance back and forth the people assembled in the encircling line shift their positions, so that all the women are on the north side and all the men on the south; then the entire body dances, with brief intervals of rest, while twelve songs are sung. The maskers next form in single file on the east, march around the fire, through the flames of which each passes the ends of his two sacred wands to destroy any lurking evil, then back around the eastern cedar tree, again around the fire, then to the southern tree, and so on to each of the four trees, when they take their leave.

This much constitutes that part of the ceremony in which the *gáŭn* are the chief participants and which usually occupies half the night. The remainder of the night is consumed by the performance of some ceremony forming the principal objective — often the puberty rite above described.

PEYOTE EXPERIENCES

A Cheyenne, forty-eight years of age, educated at Carlisle, worked in the hospital there. After leaving school he was employed in other Indian hospitals. Becoming a confirmed drunkard, according to his own statements, his chief object in life was to obtain whiskey; he would do anything for a drink. He so neglected his wife and children that others had to clothe and feed them, until his wife was finally compelled to leave him. He had no interest in his tribesmen; even should they be in distress, he was quite indifferent to their suffering. Once a man of fine physique, he became so emaciated that he weighed only one hundred and forty-five pounds. Once after a drinking debauch he was run over by a wagon and his chest crushed.

While still an invalid, friends persuaded him to join the Peyote organization. After becoming a member, he not only drank no intoxicants, but claims that the craving completely left him and that at no time does he desire to drink. Within a few years he has become one of the most substantial men of the tribe, living in a good home, with his children well cared for. He cultivates his own farm and proudly boasts that no member of his tribe can grow more wheat to the acre than he; and with greater pride asserts that if any member of his tribe is in trouble or distress, " I shall always do everything I can to help him, and that makes me happy."

A Ponca man of sixty years relates: " I was just like a skeleton; I had tuberculosis; I was almost dead, and weighed but ninety-five pounds. I went to see some white doctors. They looked at me and said: 'You are the same as dead; you should go home and die. Do not spend money to talk with doctors; save your money to buy a coffin.'

"Then my friend said, 'You had better join the Peyote; perhaps that will make you well.' I became a member of the Peyote society and took peyote all the time. Soon I grew stronger. In three months I was almost a strong man. In a year I was like a young man and had nearly doubled my weight. Before I joined the Peyote I did not care how other people lived. They might be hungry, but that did not concern me. Now I always think about other people, and all the Indians know that if they are hungry they can come to me."

Many other experiences might be related, but these are typical. There are many who, having once been confirmed drunkards, now claim that since becoming members of the Peyote order they have lost all desire to drink.

SECTION FOUR: Religion

Teton Sioux: The Vision Cry
Hopi: Deities
Nambé Tewa: Snake Cult

THE VISION CRY[1]

The father of a child seriously ill may beseech its recovery by a vow to worship the Great Mystery in fasting and prayer. First, filling his ceremonial pipe, he takes the child out under the open sky at break of day, holds it in his arms, and reverently raises the pipe aloft to the west, praying, "Great Mystery, All-powerful, permit this child of mine to recover health, and when the summer comes I will worship you with many offerings." The Vision Cry may also be observed by one desirous simply of a revelation and the gift of mystery-powers. As soon as possible the intending faster collects the materials for the promised offerings: a red-painted buffalo-robe, a calf-skin, tobacco, and kinnikinnick; all of which, wrapped in a bundle, he suspends from the tipi-lifter, where they remain until the time comes to redeem the vow.

Near the end of June he summons to his tipi, through the herald, the prominent men of the village. In silence the pipe is filled and passed about the circle. Soon the host apprises the company of his unredeemed pledge to the Mystery, and inquires if they know of a man who understands this rite. "Yes," is their response; "we know of one who is a priest of this *Haⁿbĕlĕ-cheapi*." At once he fills a pipe, bears it to the tipi of the priest, and silently extends it to him. Without a word it is accepted, lighted, and offered successively to the spirits of the Four Winds, the Sky Father, and the Earth Mother. Having smoked with deliberation, the priest speaks:

"I understand what you wish. This is my rite. I stood alone a day and a night, worshipping the Great Mystery, but it was hard. Do you wish this one day? If you do, tell me. Then I stood two days and two nights alone on a hill. That was yet harder. Do you want that? If you do, tell me. Again I stood three days and three nights,

[1] In this and in other ceremonies herein described the reader is taken back to a period when more primitive conditions existed, when the religious rites were performed in their aboriginal purity. With the gradual civilization of the tribes much of the old life has passed away, so that their ceremonies are now in most cases little more than a memory. The Foster-parent Chant is occasionally still observed, but the Vision Cry, the Sun Dance, and the rites of the Ghost Keeper have not been performed within very recent years.

crying to the Mystery, and it was very hard. Do you want that? If you do, tell me. Then I stood four days and four nights upon a hilltop, praying and crying to the spirits of Sky and Earth, to *Waká^n-ta^{n}ka*, Great Mysterious One. I drank no water and ate no food. That was the hardest of all. Do you want that? If you do, tell me."

"My heart is strong; my father's heart was strong. I have promised the Great Mystery to worship him. I will fast four days and four nights," is the response.

"It is very hard, but the Mystery will aid you. Go now to your tipi; choose two good young men and request them to build a sweat-lodge for you early in the morning."

The selection of the two *Iní-wowashi*, Sweat Workers, and the bestowal of presents upon them, end the day's preparations.

At sunrise the sweat-lodge is erected, facing the east. In the centre is a small pit to hold the heated stones, and behind this the ground is strewn with sage. Ten paces from the entrance the turf is removed from a spot designed to receive the fire and is heaped up just east of the cleared space. Firewood and twenty-five smooth round stones are gathered, and the latter, painted red by the faster, are thrown into the leaping flames. The priest enters the sweat-lodge, and, sitting in the place of honor at the rear, lays before him the bundle containing red robe, calf-skin, tobacco, and kinnikinnick. These articles he unwraps, while the faster enters and sits down at his left. He next commands the Sweat Workers to procure four young cherry stocks, in length seven or eight feet, untrimmed and not cut with axe or knife, but twisted and broken from the roots. Two buffalo-chips are laid side by side back of the stone-pit, and behind them a glowing ember, carefully borne on the prong of a fire-stick, is deposited by one of the young men. With the never-omitted motions of raising the hand to the four world-quarters, the sky, and the earth, the priest makes sacred smoke by dropping a bit of sweet-grass upon the coal, and passes the tobacco through the incense four times, to make it sacred. Having thoroughly mixed tobacco and kinnikinnick, he sanctifies the pipe by rubbing his hand downward on each of its four sides, before each movement placing the hand on the earth as if to draw its essence from it. Then with cere-monious deliberation he fills the pipe, seals it with buffalo-tallow, ties a stalk of sage about each extremity of the stem, and hands it to the faster, who places it, bowl to the westward, on the heap of turf outside.

The priest is now to prepare *waóⁿyapi*, offerings to the Great Mystery. The principal *waóⁿyapi* consists of a quantity of tobacco tied into a corner of the red robe, which is attached to a branch of one of the cherry poles. For the others fifty smaller portions of tobacco tied up in pieces of calf-skin are fastened to the twigs of the other three boughs. All four are then deposited in a row to the east of the pile of turf, the principal offering being farthest removed. Beyond this is placed a buffalo-robe, previously purified in sacred smoke. During the portion of the ceremony thus far performed — *Wakáⁿ-kághapi* (make sacred) — no one save the two young men is permitted to approach the sweat-lodge, which is *wakáⁿ*.

Priest and faster now step outside and remove their clothing, while one of the Sweat Workers calls for worthy men to come and take part in the sweat. Those who respond disrobe to the loin-cloth and follow the two principal actors into the sudatory. None may touch the faster, for he is holy. When all are seated, the priest chants a song and speaks:

"This is my rite. This young man has given me many presents and asked for *Haⁿbĕlé-cheapi*. I have worshipped the Great Mystery many times, and I now ask Thunder for a blue day. The Mystery has created many animals, some of which are like men. This young man will see them."

Continuing, he instructs the faster:

"This sweat removes from your body all evil, all touch of woman, and makes you *wakáⁿ*, that the spirit of the Great Mystery may come close to you and strengthen you. When our sweat is over, you will take pipe and buffalo-robe and go to some high mountain where the air is pure. On your return you must be careful to speak the truth in telling us of your visions, for should you deceive us, we might work you great harm in trying to aid you in interpreting the revelations sent by the Mystery."

The stones, glowing white with heat, are placed in the pit. The priest offers to the Great Mystery a small piece of dog flesh and another of dried buffalo-meat taken from a bowl of each brought by the faster's relatives, and after marking with charcoal two stripes across the inner surface of a wooden cup, he fills it with water and gives both meat and cup to the faster. The attendants close the entrance, the priest chants another song, and, bidding the faster cry, dashes water twice on the stones. After a time air is admitted; then follows another song, and more water is thrown on the stones. Twice more this is repeated, and the faster, never ceasing to cry aloud, comes forth, puts on his moccasins, takes the pipe in his left and the robe in his right hand, and starts out on his sacred journey. Behind him follow the two *Ini-wowashi* bearing the offerings.

At the foot of some lonely hill miles away from human habitation the faster halts, still crying aloud to the Great Mystery and holding the pipe before him in supplication. The two attendants pass by him and proceed to the summit, where they plant the four *waónyapi* at the corners of a square of some six or eight feet, the chief offering being, of course, to the west. Within this space they spread a thick covering of sage, for this is sacred ground and must not be touched by the feet of the suppliant.

The faster is now left alone in the presence of the Mysterious. Reverently he removes moccasins and loin-cloth, throws the robe about his shoulders, and stands with uplifted face in the centre of the sacred square, extending the pipe to the sun. At noon he turns and prays to the Mystery of the South; at sunset to Thunder, the Wing Flapper, Spirit of the West. As darkness spreads over valley, plain, and hilltop, he lies prone, with face still turned to the west, calling upon the Thunder Mystery to grant him a vision. In awe-inspiring solitude and the darkness of midnight he prays to Waziya, who sends the biting north wind and blinding snow, and who also controls in some mysterious way the movement of the buffalo. The first glimmer of dawn beholds him in the attitude of humble supplication before the deity that holds sway in the east. As the rim of the sun appears above the horizon he stands erect, clasping the shaggy buffalo-robe to his breast and offering the pipe to the orb, while with loud cries he expresses to the mysterious powers of the universe his heart's desires.

Having become *wakáⁿ*, mysterious, supernatural, by reason of the ceremonial sweat, the faster is now able to understand the speech of supernatural beings, and of animals and birds. At some time during his vigil on the hilltop one of these creatures — bird or beast, tree, rock, natural phenomenon, ghost of ancestor — appears before him, either in its own proper body or in the form of a man, and after commending his strength of heart in having endured the pangs of hunger and thirst and the temptation of evil spirits to leave the sacred spot in fright, the spirit-being reveals to him information of the future, and then, pointing out some shrub or plant, says: "There is medicine; take it, and cure your people of illness." Thus every man who has seen such a vision becomes, to a certain degree, a medicine-man; whether he uses his divinely given rites and remedies so extensively as to be known generally as a dispeller of disease, *wičhášha-wakáⁿ*, man of mystery, depends upon his own initiative. He has the medicine; it is for him to use it, much or little. The mysterious creature itself becomes the suppliant's tutelary spirit, his so-called "fighting medicine," to aid him in battle and in every crisis of life. Its image is painted upon his shield, his tipi, his gala robe, and before entering upon any undertaking of importance he beseeches its favor and guidance in prayer and song.

But not to every one that endures the pangs of the four days' fast is it given to behold a vision. While to some may be unfolded many events of the future in the course of a single fast, there are many well-known instances of a man having sought more than once in vain for a revelation of the supernatural. The truth of the vision seen is never questioned; it may be wrongly interpreted, but always subsequent events will prove that the spirit-creature was not at fault. It follows naturally that a man never feigns to have seen a vision, for such a course could result only in misleading the people and thus bringing misfortune when the sages give their interpretation.

The first day of the fast is the prototype of those that follow. If in the end the seeker after divine favor is still denied his prayer, he no longer stands with face confidently uplifted to the mysterious powers, but sinks to the ground, bowing his head upon his knees in utter dejection, and praying, aloud or in silence, to the Spirits of the West, the North, the East, the South, the Sky, and the Earth. His eyes are downcast, averted from the face of the Great Mystery in the sky until his appeal is granted and the revelation given, or until he has relinquished all hope, knowing that in some way he has offended the divine ones and that the power of the supernatural, for the present at least, is denied him.

When the proper time has elapsed, the two attendants return to the hill, mounted, and leading a horse for the faster, who, weak and emaciated from hunger, thirst, and lack of sleep, is lifted bodily to the animal's back and supported as the horse is led slowly homeward. The trio halt in front of the sweat-lodge, into which the priest and a helper bear the faster, still clasping his pipe. The old men, anxious to hear the story of his visions, quickly disrobe and enter. The faster can now detect a disagreeable human odor, for he is holy, and human flesh, however clean, has for him a peculiar smell. The priest takes the pipe from his hands, removes the tallow, and, looking into the bowl, says:

"There is nothing in it. What have you done that the pipe is empty?"

"I do not know," answers the faster.

"The Mysteries," solemnly announces the priest, "have smoked this pipe. Tell us, my friend, truthfully all that you have seen."

The vision, if one has been experienced, is then described, and, unless its significance is obvious, is interpreted by the priest and the sages. A cup of water and a piece of meat, both having first been purified by exposure to the incense of sweet-grass and offered to the Mysteries by the priest, are given to the faster, and the sweat now takes place as on the first morning.

On the distant hilltop remain standing the four withered boughs bearing the robe and the little bags of sacred tobacco, offerings to the mysterious, the infinite, the incomprehensible powers of sky and earth.

RELIGION

The principal Hopi deities are the following:

1. Kafsínamǔ (singular, Kafsína). The Kachinas are supernatural, anthropomorphic beings inhabiting the water-world that underlies the earth. While a certain spring called Kisíu-va [1] is regarded as their home, they are believed to be present also in all other bodies of living water, the Hopi conception being that all bodies of water are parts of one great ocean underlying the earth, in other words, mere openings through the earth-crust into the water-world. In ancient times these beings sometimes appeared to the people, but when they did so they always wore masks made of yucca-leaves. The first Kachinas were visible beings of supernatural power, but because the people did not treat them with consideration they became invisible. They are now represented by masked dancers. Certain clan legends represent the ancestors of those clans as having been Kachinas who gave up their supernatural attributes and became mere human beings. All Hopi boys and many girls are initiated into the Kachina order and thus become capable of participating as masked Kachinas in the various summer dances. This initiation of children, occurring as a part of the Powámǔ ceremony, is elsewhere described.[2] The Kachinas are of numerous kinds, the most important being:

(a) Léna Kafsínamǔ ("flute Kachinas").

(b) Kúwan Kafsínamǔ ("all-colors Kachinas").

(c) Muzíwus Kafsínamǔ ("beans Kachinas").

(d) Ká'na Kafsínamǔ, or Yěho Kafsínamǔ ("throwing Kachinas," so called because they throw boiled corn among the spectators). Their songs begin with the word *Ká'na*, hence the first name. They dance only in the evening after the daylight dancing of the others.

(e) Hehéa Kafsínamǔ (*hehéa*, a nickname applied to uxorious men). These Kachinas are represented as being very fond of women.

(f) Kóyěmsi Kafsínamǔ, or Tafsókta Kafsínamǔ ("knob-head Kachinas," in allusion to the peculiar protuberances on their masks, which completely envelope the head). They correspond to the Zuñi Kóyěmǎshi, and it would be difficult indeed to distinguish between a Zuñi and a Hopi mask.

---

[1] Kisíu-va ("shadow spring") is on the east side of the timbered hills to the northeast of Walpi, the spot being known as Kísiuû ("shadow place") on account of the shade cast by perpendicular rocks about the spring.

(g) Tŭmas Kaʦínamŭ ("female Kachinas").

(h) Hahaíi Kaʦínamŭ (so-named in allusion to their cry). These last two kinds are called the "mothers of all the Kachinas," but thus far no myth shedding light on the epithet has been discovered.

(i) Tûnwŭp Kaʦínamŭ ("whipping Kachinas"). These ceremonially whip the children at their initiation into the Kachina order.

(j) Héĕ Kaʦínamŭ. These are personated by women dressed as warriors.

(k) Tûváʦ Kaʦínamŭ ("weeping Kachinas"). These always weep after speaking.

(l) Kŏkölĕ Kaʦínamŭ (so named in allusion to their peculiar cry).

(m) Powámŭ Kaʦínamŭ. These are called the "uncles of all the Kachinas."

(n) Wiyákötĕ Kaʦínamŭ. These also are described as "uncles of the Kachinas."

(o) Natáaska Kaʦínamŭ.

(p) Soyál Kaʦínamŭ. These appear only in the winter solstice ceremony, Soyálanû.

(q) Aná Kaʦínamŭ ("long-hair Kachinas").

(r) Cháqaina Kaʦínamŭ.

(s) Wawáʃh Kaʦínamŭ ("running Kachinas"). These pursue and punish in various ways those spectators who attempt to escape with food brought into the plaza by the Kachinas. See pages 199. 203.

(t) Náa'mû Kaʦínamŭ.

(u) Súyuk Kaʦínamŭ ("ogress Kachinas").

Many other Kachinas have been added by late borrowing from other pueblos, such as Zuñi, Jemez, and other eastern settlements. Recently a number of Kachinas have been invented by individual Hopi; and this doubtless is a result of the universal desire among primitive people for masked characters. It is not to be believed that a man could deliberately create a dog mask or a sheep mask, as has been done recently, and persuade himself that there are any supernatural beings among the Kachinas whom these masks represent. Even Pahána (American) Kaʦína appears in the dances of today.

It is firmly believed that the Kachinas dwell in Kisíu-va. Sometimes the people who visit this spring see what they believe to be evidences that the Kachina children have been making mud piki, in the same manner as human children, and occasionally they see finger-prints on the walls of rock.

2. Táwa, the Sun, is considered to be the father of all life. Every Hopi utters or "thinks" a morning prayer and offers cornmeal to the rising Sun, asking for long life without sickness. Chiefs pray for all the people, while others pray only for themselves. The Sun is the principal deity worshipped in the winter solstice ceremony, which was brought to the Hopi country by the Cloud clan and others from the south.

3. Múyôŭ, the Moon, is the Father who guards the people at night. He is not especially worshipped in a ceremony, but any individual in trouble makes pahos for many deities, including the Moon, and deposits them in various unprescribed places.

4. Sótûû, the Stars, are regarded as supernatural beings. Until about 1890 the taboo on drinking water at meals was commonly observed; and when the desire to drink became imperative, one went outside and with uplifted face — "inhaled the spirit of the stars," and thus made oneself strong. When a Hopi happens to pass near a spring in which the stars are reflected, he takes a drink from it for the same purpose. In the winter solstice ceremony pahos are made for the Stars and the Moon, and individuals starting on a journey make pahos for them in order that these deities may guard the travellers at night.

5. Sótŭkunani ("star rain god") is a sky deity especially besought for rain. He is a supreme being to whom prayers are offered for general and specific benefactions of all kinds. He is not identified with any visible object, but is said to dwell above, and is sometimes called Óvĕ-monwi ("above chief").

6. Múinwa, a god of germination, dwells underground, and having no particular shrine, is supplicated in any place for good crops. Átkyak-monwi ("nadir chief") is said to be another name for the same deity. He is represented as a very large man with a body made up of all the edible fruits and seeds. A successful farmer is said to be a "Múinwa man."

7. Nayánap-tûmsi ("all-kinds-of-seeds clanswoman") is another deity concerned with the germination of seeds. As the wife of Múinwa she lives with him beneath the ground, and both are supplicated by those who especially desire bountiful crops. Like all other supernatural beings they receive prayer-sticks at the winter solstice ceremony.

8. Nalónanŭ-monwitŭ ("four chiefs") are rain gods presiding at the four solstitial points, that is, the points on the horizon marked by the rising and setting sun at the summer and the winter solstice. Sótŭkunani, the sky god, is the rain god of the zenith, but apparently Múinwa takes the place of the nadir deity. Pahos made for these gods are deposited at springs, the suppliant choosing a spring at each of the solstitial points. One going on a journey makes pahos for these deities and places them all in one spring in the direction of his destination. The North Chief controls the cold, and the north wind (*qínyôŭ;* cf. *qiní'wika,* northward) is his breath. These deities manifest themselves to the eye in the form of clouds.

9. Halákvû, or Tûvíp-haiyanû, is the whirlwind. The name Halákvû refers to the rattling noise made by the rubbish carried along by a whirlwind; Tûvíp-haiyanû to the whirling motion itself. In every ceremony this deity is supplicated that he may remain peaceful and quiet, and permit the ceremony to be finished in good weather. Pahos or *naqáqŭsi* are always made for him, but there is no particular shrine at which they are deposited. Warriors ask him to become active, that they may the more easily approach their enemy unseen.

10. Másôŭ grants both good and evil petitions. When the first clans came into the Walpi country he was a supernatural in human, visible form, dwelling on the spot where Kuchaptuvela afterward was built; but he soon disappeared and became a spirit. His ancient home among the rocks below the mesa is now his shrine. Másôŭ is one of the principal deities worshipped in the winter solstice ceremony, and indeed few, if any, are to be ranked above him. In a way not yet clearly understood he is connected with fire. He is also in a sense a god of the dead, his name being used as the term for corpse; but the connection here lies merely in the fact that both Másôŭ and the spirits of the dead inhabit the underground region. Most important of all, Másôŭ is a god of germination; and here the connecting idea seems to be the conception that the growth of plants is dependent on warmth, and warmth is the product of fire.

Probably the best statement of the position of Másôŭ in Hopi mythology is that he is the *genius loci* in very much the way this phrase was understood by the Romans. He is a beneficent spirit, and answers the requests of all who in the prescribed manner pray for good crops, long life, and health. But also he grants the desires of those who pray for evil purposes; hence he formerly was much supplicated by sorcerers. To summarize: while the several conceptions of the function of Másôŭ are not perfectly clear, perhaps not even to the Hopi themselves, it is quite plain that his chief function is the care of germinating seeds and growing crops.

All the deities mentioned above receive attention in every Hopi ceremony. The following however are supplicated only on special occasions.

11. Tihkûyi, or Tûwá-poṇ-tûmsi ("earth around clanswoman"), is a female deity who gave birth to all the species of game animals, from rabbits to elk. Offerings are left at her shrine in the winter solstice ceremony, that she may increase the supply of game, and when a hunting party is organized she is requested to give the hunters permission to kill her children.

12. Pökáṇ-hoya (*pökaṇ*, meaning unknown; *hóya*, little) and Palóṇao-hoya ("echo little"), his younger twin, are the boy war gods. Two gods bearing these names live in the crater of Zuñi Salt lake, and two others at Óṇ-tûpka ("salt cañon") in the Grand cañon, each pair with its grandmother, Spider Woman. When the Hopi make prayer-sticks or *naqáqŭsi* for the warrior gods at the Salt lake, they deposit them on the east side of the pueblo, and when the offerings are intended for those at the Salt cañon they are placed on the west side of the mesa. The exigencies of story-telling have resulted in the invention of many other homes for the warrior gods, but these two places are the only homes recognized in ceremonies. The twin gods are supplicated for courage, and because of their indifference to suffering, they are requested to visit the North Chief and have him send cold weather, which brings snow and resultant moisture for the fields. As there are numerous myths describing the manner in which the brothers extricated people from all kinds of difficulties, so in actual life they are besought with pahos and prayers to help the sufferer out of his worst troubles. In mythology the war gods travel on the rainbow, or on the downy feather of an eagle, and thus move about with almost instantaneous rapidity. They understand the language of all creatures, and know all the secrets of medicines to cure sickness. They have great power, not only against ordinary human beings, but even against sorcerers, whom they outwit by becoming invisible and concealing themselves behind an invisible but impenetrable barrier; so that the sorcerers, though they also can assume invisibility, can do no harm to the war gods because their missiles of *sucháva* (Olivella shells) are checked by the unseen wall. Two wooden (?) figurines of the war gods are kept in a shrine on the southern slope of a mesa south of Walpi, and are taken thence to Mishongnovi for the approximately quadrennial initiation of Wŭwûtŝimŭ. Another pair, made of stone, is kept in a niche in the Walpi Warrior Fraternity house.

13. Tála-tûmsi ("dawn clanswoman"),[1] a deity supplicated only in the new fire ceremony, is said to be a personification of the female principle. Since women are not admitted to the kiva during the new fire ceremony, the image of the goddess, when brought to Qán-kiva, is set on the roof during a certain number of days, while the initiates are within. She thus typifies the godmother called in to officiate at the birth of a child. While the image sits on the roof, women throw meal toward it and pray to the goddess that they may have children and bear them without pain.

14. Naná-mana ("cornsmut girl") has a shrine at the left of the trail from Walpi to Middle mesa. Like many other shrines it contains a piece of petrified wood. These objects, being somewhat uncommon in this region, are placed in shrines simply to mark them as unusual places, and have no special religious significance. There is a myth relating how Naná-mana, after bidding the people pray to her for good crops, disappeared at the place now marked by the shrine.

15. Ón-wûhti ("salt woman") is supplicated with offerings at two shrines, one at "Salt cañon" in the Grand cañon, the other near the Salt lake of the Zuñi. Suppliants pray that they may obtain the salt easily, saying, for instance, "We offer these prayers to you that you may keep the salt pure, and let us get it easily." The warrior gods also receive similar petitions from the salt gatherers.

16. Pá-lölökanû ("water bullsnake") is the personification of the water-spirit. This is the so-called "plumed serpent." The cult was brought from the south by the Cloud clan, and another phase of the same cult was imported by the Tansy-mustard clan and other Tewa people from the Rio Grande valley. The earth is believed to be underlaid by a world of water, and springs are mere openings, or eyes as the Spanish call them, leading out of the water-world. Although the Water Bullsnake inhabits the lower world, while his power is everywhere and offerings to him may be made in any spring, still the spring Tawá-pa is regarded as the real home of Pá-lölökanû. Images of the Water Bullsnake are exhibited in any Kachina ceremony in February and March, and sometimes in the winter solstice ceremony.

17. Kókyan-wûhti ("spider woman") is prominent in myths, playing the part of fairy godmother and is possessed of almost unlimited power. She is the grandmother of the twin warrior gods,

---

[1] While Fewkes's translation of "Dawn Woman" has been used here, no informant interviewed would concede the translation. Dawn is talávaiya, while tála is daylight, or a period of twenty-four hours. There seems to be no reason for questioning the translation, in spite of the dissent of informants.

and appears sometimes in human form, sometimes in the form of various animals, but more often as a spider. In opposing sorcery she assumes the spider form and bids the one whom she is defending to place her behind his ear, from which position she directs his acts. Prayers for help are offered to Spider Woman at any time.

There is no doubt that the Tewa and probably other Pueblos formerly and within recent years kept large rattlesnakes in captivity as creatures to be venerated and propitiated. Whether the custom still persists, and whether human sacrifice was made to the reptiles, which many native informants declare to have been the case, cannot be proved. The evidence regarding this cult is necessarily fragmentary, but the witnesses are surprisingly numerous considering the danger attending revelations of this sort. Besides the following quotations, additional evidence bearing on snake worship will be given as applying to Nambé. All the statements of natives were recorded in 1909. Prior to that time the only published references to the cult had appeared in the writings of Bandelier: [1]

The Sa-jiu [2] . . . is the keeper, in every village where the office exists, of a greenish liquid called "Frog water," . . . which the Indians use as an infallible remedy against snake bites. . . . The common belief in New Mexico, that the Pueblo Indians keep, or at least kept until recently, enormous rattlesnakes in their villages, treating them, if not with veneration, at least with particular care, is not unfounded. Gigantic rattlesnakes are killed now and then, — animals of enormous size. One of these, six feet long, was killed on the lower Rio Grande last year. In 1884, a rattlesnake, the body of which I saw myself, was killed at San Juan. It measured over seven feet in length. Tracks of gigantic snakes, or trails rather, have been met often. I saw a fresh one in the mountains west of Santa Fé that indicated a very large serpent. But the Indians, though generally reticent concerning these facts, have confessed to me that there exists among the Tehuas a special office of "Keeper of the Snake." This office is in near relation with that of the Sa-jiu, and under her quasi control. Until not long ago (and perhaps to-day) eight large rattlesnakes were kept in a house at San Juan alive, very secretly, and it was the Po-a-nyu, or keeper, who had them in charge. When the one that I saw was killed, five years ago, the Indians of the pueblo showed both displeasure and alarm.

It is positively asserted that the Pecos adored, and the Jemez and Taos still adore, an enormous rattlesnake, which they keep alive in some inaccessible and hidden mountain recess. It is even dimly hinted at that human sacrifices might be associated with this already sufficiently hideous cult. . . . It has always been the natural tendency . . . to make bad look worse and good better than it actually is. . . . I have previously mentioned that Ruiz had been called upon

---

[1] *Papers Archæological Institute of America*, III, 1890, pages 305–307; I, 1883, page 126.
[2] Sá^{n}shu^n, head of the women who are not members of a society.   The present writer has no information regarding the connection of this personage with the snake cult.

by the Indians of Pecos to do his duty by attending to the sacred fire for one year, and that he refused. The reason . . . appears to have been that there was a belief to the effect that anyone who had ever attended to the embers would, if he left the tribe, die without fail. Even Ruiz affirmed that the tale, so far as the Pecos were concerned, was certainly true. He never could get to see the reptile, however. It was a rattlesnake (*Cascabel*).

Mariano Ruiz, from whom Bandelier derived information about Pecos customs, was a Mexican who as a boy became so intimate with the Indians that he was later adopted by them and when the pueblo was abandoned in 1838 he received such of the community land as was not sold. In 1924 an effort was made to obtain from the Mexicans now living near Pecos ruin such traditions as they might have preserved regarding the snake cult. Through the good offices of Mrs. Adelina Otero-Warren a man who, as it happened, was the grandson of Ruiz, was induced to repeat what he had heard his grandfather tell about the Pecos snake; and a dramatic recital it was. The snake, he said, was kept in an underground room in the village, and at stated intervals a newborn infant was fed to it. The elder Ruiz was asked to assume the duty of custodian of the sacred fire, an annual office, which he declined because he had observed that the fire-keeper always died soon after being released from confinement in the subterranean chamber where the fire burned. (Whether the fire and the serpent were housed in the same cell the grandson did not know, but possibly such was the case and the refusal of Ruiz to accept the proffered position was really due to his horror at the idea of spending a year in proximity to the reptile. But there appears to be no good reason why he should not have imparted this information to Bandelier, if such was the case.) Strolling about the environs of the village, Ruiz one day came upon his most intimate friend bowed in grief. To the Mexican's inquiry the Indian responded that his newborn child had been condemned to be fed to the snake, that already he had been forced to yield several children to the sacrifice, and had vainly hoped that this one would be spared. This was the first time Ruiz had heard that children were fed to the snake. He proposed that they hoodwink the priests, and acting on his advice the Indian poisoned a newborn kid with certain herbs, wrapped it up as if it were a baby, and threw it to the reptile. That night terrifying sounds issued from the den as the great snake writhed in its death agony, and in the morning it lay with the white of its belly exposed. The populace was utterly downcast, for this presaged the extinction of the tribe.[1]

About the year 1913 Mrs. Matilda Coxe Stevenson published in a New Mexico newspaper certain information she had received from a San Ildefonso man regarding Tewa snake worship, especially mentioning the subject of human sacrifice. Her informant was promptly executed by a Keres delegation from Santo Domingo, and such a stringent ban was placed on further revelations of ceremonies that it is now more than ever difficult to induce natives to discuss such subjects, especially the snake cult. Mrs. Stevenson's data have not been published, but the following generalizations appeared:

The most shocking ceremony associated with the zooic worship of the Tewa is the propitiation of the rattlesnake with human sacrifice to prevent further destruction from the venomous bites of the reptile. The greatest secrecy is observed and the ceremonies are performed without the knowledge of the people except those directly associated with the rite which is performed quadrennially. Although many legends of the various Pueblos have pointed indirectly to human sacrifice in the past, it was a revelation to Mrs. Stevenson when she was informed that this rite was observed by the Tewa at the present time; and, while it is said to exist only in two of the villages, she has reason to believe that they are not exceptions. In one village the subject is said to be the youngest female infant; in the other village an adult woman is reported to be sacrificed, a woman without husband or children being selected whenever possible. The sacrificial ceremonies occur in the kiva. The subjects are drugged with *Datura meteloides* until life is supposed to be extinct. At the proper time the body is placed upon a sand painting on the floor before the table altar and the ceremony proceeds amid incantations and strange performances. The infant is nude, and the woman is but scantily clad. After the flesh has decomposed and nothing but the bones remain the skeleton is deposited, with offerings, beneath the floor of an adjoining room of the kiva. The entire ceremony is performed with the greatest solemnity.

The details of the alleged sacrifice, as given in the preceding quotation, are unconfirmed.

A San Juan man, whose name must of course remain secret, says:

[1] If Ruiz really had a hand in doing away with the Pecos snake, he of course would not have revealed the fact to Bandelier, for publication of such a confession would very likely have been his death warrant, even though Pecos itself had been abandoned for forty years. The tradition is here recorded for what it may be worth. The most the writer can say for it is that there seems to be nothing inherently impossible in it.

When I was a youth of about fourteen I herded my father's
cattle. It was in the month of August, and just after midday. Going
down an arroyo I saw a track as if someone had been dragging a
heavy log. Some small bushes were broken. I followed it to see
who was dragging this log. It was strange that the track was not in
a straight line. I went up on a small hillock to see where the cattle
were, and I was just about to jump down the slope on the other side,
when I saw in front of me under an overhanging rock a very large
snake. I could not run. It was coiled. It had an arrow-head mark
on the back of its head and smaller ones on its body. Its head was
raised. It did not rattle. It seemed a long time before I could jump
back and run home to tell my father and uncle. They did not believe
me, and would not go back with me to see. A short time after this a
Frenchman was quarrying rock for Samuel Eldodt, and while he
was cooking he heard a sound like a man snoring. He investigated,
and in a cave saw a big snake. He killed it. He told my society
brother about it, and that is how I know. He brought the snake to
Eldodt, and only one Indian was allowed to see it. This was Luis
Kata, who is now dead. There was no excitement among the Indians,
only surprise that there could be such a large snake.

The last sentence of the statement was in reply to a direct question.
The San Juan snake was killed in 1884 by a Frenchman quarrying rock. He was cooking his supper, and the snake came to the
door of his cabin. Almost paralyzed with fright, he seized a sharp
pinch-bar and struck. The bar passed through its neck, but the
snake was so large that the implement simply punctured instead of
severing it. To make sure that it was dead he cut the body in three
pieces with a shovel, and then came to San Juan and informed
Samuel Eldodt, who went to the quarry and brought it home in a
large packing-case. They found the place from which the snake had
come, a small cave in the rocks walled in with stones and pots.
The village that night was in an uproar, and Eldodt, though thoroughly familiar with the Indians and not given to false alarms, was
uncertain that he and his household would live through the night.
The snake was seven feet six inches long and "as thick as a stove-
pipe." [1]
The positive denial of the native informant quoted above that
there was any excitement in the village after this occurrence is good
proof that in denying the existence of snake worship at San Juan he
is equally disingenuous. Both Eldodt and Bandelier, who saw the
snake after it was killed, testify to the intense excitement of the

[1] Information from Samuel Eldodt, 1924.

Indians. The discovery of the man-made den of the serpent sheds light on the refusal of the old men of the pueblo to accompany the boy back to the place where he saw the reptile: realizing that it had escaped from its den, and unwilling that a child should know this secret, they doubtless went out secretly and drove it back.

Another San Juan man says:

Snakes were formerly kept in the hills and fed by the people of the village. There were two snakes, but one went away and was lost, the other was killed by a man who was quarrying rock in the hills east of San Juan. It was so large that he became afraid to stay there afterward. The Indians were much incensed that the snake had been killed. It was fed tortillas and meat by Juan Pedro twice daily, early in the morning and late in the afternoon. There used to be a man here who, on seeing a snake, would wave his hat over the reptile until it became passive and could be handled.

An old Mexican who as a boy spent so much of his time among the San Juan Indians that he still, in 1909, spoke the language like a native, said that he once accompanied two playmates on burros to a wild nook in the hills, where his companions threw meal and small tortillas bearing the snake symbol into a small cave filled with a writhing mass of rattlesnakes.

Some years ago freshet water rushing down the acequia flooded the village of Santa Clara. Early in the morning a white neighbor, entering the village to secure help in repairing her roof, found the men crowded about a kiva at the edge of the elevation on which the pueblo stands. Some were bailing water from the subterranean room. They motioned her away, and appeared greatly concerned lest she approach closer. The man she sought said that he could by no means leave at the moment. Some time after this she was told that the Santa Clara snakes had been drowned; and though her informant did not say that the event had taken place at the time of the flood, the supposition is that such was the fact.[1]

In 1924 the same observer saw in the road a mile or two from Santa Clara a rattlesnake gaily decorated with stripes of red paint. This recalls the Zuñi custom of adorning a rattlesnake caught in a cultivated field and releasing it outside with supplications for its good-will.

---

[1] Terrestrial snakes of course are not helpless in water; but the captives may have been too closely confined to keep their heads above water, or they may have been so recently fed as to be too torpid to swim.

The Santa Clara Indians say that by inserting into a snake's mouth the tip of a twig moistened with saliva they can render the reptile unconscious. In order to convince a skeptical American neighbor a young man caught a non-venomous snake, secured a toothpick, placed the tip in his mouth and then in the snake's mouth, which he distended by pressing a forked stick on its neck. The reptile almost at once became lethargic, and soon was as motionless and limp as a piece of rope. It lay in the patio some hours before disappearing unnoticed.

SECTION FIVE: Historical Accounts

The Papago

THE PAPAGO

THE Papago are a strong branch of the Piman family living in the narrow valleys of south-central Arizona as far north as Tucson, and the broad desert stretches of northern Sonora. They were among the first of the Indians of this section to come under the influence of the Spanish missionaries, and early proved their friendliness toward Christianity; that is, as with Indians generally, so far as its outward form is concerned. The Papago certainly proved tractable enough, under the efforts of the Franciscans, to build one of the most beautiful mission churches in the United States, and while all similar edifices of the region have fallen into decay, they have kept this wonderful old structure at San Xavier del Bac in a good state of preservation.

The recorded history of the village of Bac, situated ten miles south of Tucson, may be said to begin with 1692, in September of which year the celebrated German Jesuit missionary, Father Eusebio Kino, or Kuehne, visited the spot. He probably again visited it two years later, as he certainly did in 1697, in January and November. It was perhaps in this year that the saint name San Xavier was first given. The population of the settlement at that time was 830 persons, living in 176 houses, being the largest village in all Pimería, as the southern Arizona country was then called. In the autumn of 1699, and again in the spring of 1700, the indomitable Jesuit was again at Bac, late in April or early in May of which latter year he founded a church, although it is not impossible that some beginning was made at the time of his next preceding visit. Kino died in 1710; but even without the guiding spirit of its founder the mission prospered until the Pima uprising of 1751, when the building was sacked by the natives, but was reoccupied in 1753. Twenty-two Jesuit padres served San Xavier from 1720 to 1767 (in which latter year the Jesuits were expelled from Mexico), followed in 1768 by Fray Francisco Garcés, its first Franciscan. In the period from 1760 to 1764 the population reached 399, but by 1772 it had dwindled to 270. In 1783 the erection of the present edifice was begun, the work continuing for fourteen years, until 1797, — the date still legible over the entrance. The mission records reveal the names of Balthasar Cavillo, from May 22, 1780, to 1794, and Narciso Gutierres, from 1794 to 1799, so that there is every probability that this noteworthy structure was begun by the former and finished during the ministration of the latter friar. In 1822 their bones were removed from Tumacacori, where they had died, and reinterred in the church that still stands as a monument to their zeal.

The following description of the church is quoted from the late Archbishop J. B. Salpointe's "Soldiers of the Cross," 1898:

"This church, as can be seen by its arches exceeding the semicircle in height, and the ornamental work in half relief which covers the flat surface of some parts of its inside walls, belongs to the Moorish style.

"The first thing to be noticed is the space formerly occupied by the atrium, a little square 66 by 33 feet, which was enclosed in front of the church, and was used, as we have seen, for holding meetings relating to matters not directly connected with religion. The walls of this place crumbled down a few years ago. On the front, which shows the width of the church with its two towers, is placed in relief the coat-of-arms of the Order of St. Francis of Assisi, the founder of the Franciscans. It consists of an escutcheon, with a white ground filled in with a twisted cord, a part of the Franciscan dress, and a cross on which are nailed one arm of Our Saviour and one of St. Francis, representing the union of the disciple with the divine Master, in charity and the love of suffering. The arm of our Lord is bare, while that of St. Francis is covered. On the right side of the escutcheon is the monogram of Jesus the Saviour of man, and on the left that of the Blessed Virgin Mary. The front was surmounted by a life-size statue of St. Francis, which has now almost gone to pieces, under the action of time.

"The church, which is built of stone and brick, is 105 by 27 feet clear inside the walls. Its form is that of a cross, the transept forming on each side of the nave a chapel of 21 feet square. The edifice has only one nave, which is divided into six portions marked by as many arches, each one resting on two pillars set against the walls. Above the transept is a cupola of about fifty feet in elevation, the remainder of the vaults in the church being only about thirty feet high.

"Going from the front door to the main altar, there is on the right-hand side wall a fresco representing the coming of the Holy Ghost upon the disciples; opposite to it is the picture, also in fresco, of the Last Supper. Both paintings measure about 9 by 5 feet. In the first chapel to the right hand are two altars, one facing the nave with the image of Our Lady of Sorrows standing at the foot of a large cross, which is deeply engraved in the wall, and the other one with the image of the Immaculate Conception. In the same chapel are two frescoes representing Our Lady of the Rosary and the hidden life of Our Saviour. The opposite chapel is also adorned with two altars. One of them is dedicated to the Passion of our Lord, and the other to St. Joseph. There are also two paintings, the subjects of which are: Our Lady of the Pillar and the Presentation of Our Lord in the Temple.

"The main altar, which stands at the head of the church facing the nave, is dedicated to St. Francis Xavier, the patron saint the Jesuits had chosen for the first church they had established in the mission. Above the image of St. Francis Xavier is that of the Holy Virgin, between the statues of St. Peter and St. Paul, and at the summit of the altar-piece, a bust meant to represent God the Creator. The pictures on the walls near this altar are: On the right-hand side, 'The Adoration of the Wise Men' with 'The Flight into

Egypt,' and on the left, 'The Adoration of the Shepherds' with 'The Annunciation.'

"The altars, and especially the principal one, are decorated with columns and a great profusion of arabesques in low relief, all gilded or painted in different colors, according to the requirements of the Moorish style.

"Besides the images we have mentioned, there were yet in 1866, when we visited the mission for the first time, the statues of the twelve apostles, placed in the niches cut in the pillars of the church, and other statues representing saints, most of them of the Order of St. Francis. Many of them have since been broken, and the pieces removed to the vestry room. There are in the dome of the cupola the pictures in fresco of several personages of the Order, who occupied high rank in the Church.

"Going again to the front door, there are two small doors communicating with the towers. The first room on the right, in the inside of the tower, is about twelve feet square, and contains the baptismal font. A similar room, of no particular use now, but which corresponds to the mortuary chapel of the old basilicas, is formed by the inside square of the opposite tower. From each of these rooms commence the stairs, cut in the thickness of the walls and leading to the upper stories. Starting from the baptistery, the second flight reaches the choir of the church. A good view of the upper part of the church can be had from that place. There are also some frescoes worth noticing. These are the Holy Family, facing the main altar; St. Francis, represented as rapt up by heavenly love, in a fiery chariot; St. Dominic, receiving from the Blessed Virgin the mission of promoting the devotion of the Rosary in the world; and the four Evangelists, with their characteristic attributes. Two flights more lead to the belfry, where there are four home-made bells, of small size but very harmonious. Twenty-two steps more bring the visitor to the top story and under the little dome covering the tower, an elevation about seventy-five feet above the ground. Here a glance can be cast on the beautiful and extensive valley of the Santa Cruz River and on the surrounding country."

The church and mission stand on a slight elevation overlooking the lower valley, dotted with the little farms of the Papago. These people are strictly agriculturists, their principal crops being wheat and barley, which they plant in midwinter and harvest in spring. Few of them live on their farms, nearly all having their homes in the village near the mission. Outwardly they are far advanced in what is called civilization, and are professed members of the church; but the student does not find it difficult to see that overalls do not make civilization, nor baptism Christianity. In acknowledging the Christian faith the Papago merely follow the line of least resistance, for by adding a little more ceremony to their life, even if it be the ceremony of the white man, they do no violence to their primitive religion, and at the same time escape the danger of punishment by fire and brimstone threatened them in a Christian hereafter.

The larger part of the Papago are semi-nomadic; that is, they wander from place to place as occasion necessitates. One week they may be harvesting their little crops of grain; the next they have taken the trail to the mines to work for a time, or gone to the hills or river valleys to gather cactus fruit or mesquite beans. Many of them in the Fresnal valley have cattle upon which they depend wholly for support; others till small desert farms, irrigated with freshet water. Little settlements depending on scanty crops and small herds are scattered throughout south-central Arizona and northwestern Sonora.

The native houses at the Papago village of San Xavier del Bac consist almost entirely of rectangular huts of adobe mud filled in between posts and wattle. A few of the old-time circular houses are also seen there, and the scattered bands build this type almost exclusively. For summer they require only a brush shelter to protect them from the blazing sun.

Nothing of food value escaped the keen eye of the primitive Papago. Seeds of many plants, the fruit of several varieties of cactus, and mesquite beans, mescal, and tuberous roots were supplemented with various game animals and birds. The bear was never killed nor eaten, for it was believed once to have been human.

The basketry of the Papago, though somewhat less skilfully made, resembles that of their Pima cousins, as does also their pottery. They make practically all their own earthenware utensils, which with use soon change from their original bright red color to the black of old iron pots.

There are five gentile groups, though it can hardly be said that any strict gentile organization now exists. Children belong to the father's group. The creation myth tells how, when Chüwŭtŭmáka's destroying horde marched up into this world from the east, the first to come were those who were to call their fathers Ápap; then came those whose fathers were to be Apk, Mam, Vaf, and Ákulĭ respectively. These names were no doubt totemic in their origin, but only the first and third can be identified. Ápap is associated with the coyote, Mam with the buzzard. There is no general word for father; to each individual "father" is simply the name of his gens, if such groups may be so called. A member of the Apk gens, for instance, calls his father nyŭapkĭ, of the Mam gens, nyŭmam, nyŭ meaning "my." Collectively the members of the gentes are called Apápakam, Ápkĭkam, Mámakam, Váfakam, and Ákulĭkam.

Of so little importance are the gentes that marriage within them is not prohibited, or even regarded as unusual. Marriage arrangements in early days were rather peculiar in that acceptance or refusal lay with the father of the young man. When a girl became of marriageable age, her father found a suitable young man and went to his parents to arrange the match. If the girl seemed satisfactory to the youth's father, during the next four nights he instructed his son in the duties of a husband, and on the fifth sent him to the home of the girl, where he warmed himself by the fire, saying nothing. He remained there all night, returning home early in the morning. This was repeated three times; then the girl and her father went to the youth's house, where she was formally intrusted to his care. If, in their married life, the husband made accusation of infidelity against his wife, she was brought before the head-chief and publicly arraigned. The husband might refuse to take her back, in which event she became an outcast. If, however, he consented to receive her, relying on her promise not to err again, she was publicly whipped on the bare back.

Each branch or band of the Papago had its chief, whose principal assistant, selected by himself, was a herald or crier. Each also had a council, to which all adult men were admitted, and which decided all matters of importance. The office of chief was hereditary, but the succession was always confirmed by the council. The chief's duties were by no means nominal; he had to keep peace among his people and inflict punishment on the guilty. One of his principal responsibilities was to see that parents called their children long before daylight, for the Apache always made their attacks just before dawn and it was necessary to be ever on the alert. The parents were also required to see that the children went to bed early, and each morning both boys and girls practised running, that they might be swift of foot either in retreat or in pursuit.

The Papago dead were wrapped in cotton blankets, wound with rope, and buried, in the same manner as the Pima, in a niche under the side of the grave. Sometimes the body was taken to the mountains, where it was laid upon the ground, surrounded with a rude stone wall about four feet high, and covered with brush, logs, and stones. The crier for the chief was always buried in this way, but in a sitting posture, with the lower part of his face painted red and the upper part white. In front of him were placed charred ends of firewood, representing the council fire, as if he were talking to the people. Some of the deceased's best horses were killed, his property was burned, and food scattered about in the house.

The medicine-men receive their power through dreams direct from divine sources, and are considered by the people god-taught. Failure to cure disease is not taken to mean that the medicine-man has not the power to heal, but rather that he has made malign use of it. This explains the practice of destroying unsuccessful medicine-men. Disease first came through the anger of Chüwŭtŭmáka, who left it as a curse to the people as he descended into the under-world; but in compensation he placed medicine stones in the mountains and commanded the spirits of animals to instruct men how to effect cures. To a young man destined to be a medicine-man come four dreams on as many successive nights, followed on four other nights by the appearance of an animal, who speaks to him,— not an apparition, but a real animal. At the fourth appearance the young man is commanded to arise and follow; his spirit is led through four mountains, and shown what medicine is there to be found. Then the animal changes itself into a small pebble, which the young man supposedly swallows, and in later years, when all other means of expelling sickness have failed, he pretends to bring up this stone and by incantation to transform it into a spirit animal, which lends him potent aid.

In treating sickness the medicine-man uses a rattle, eagle feathers, cigarettes of native tobacco, and medicine songs. The songs and the smoke enable him to detect the seat of the disease, which he at once begins to remove by sucking. Singing, smoking, and waving of the eagle feathers continue throughout the night, and in the morning he asserts that a certain animal has caused the sickness, advising that some man who knows the songs of that animal be brought in to sing them.

The medicine-man is known by the name of the animal which instructed him, as, Medicine-man of the Eagle, Medicine-man of the Bear. In case of war the medicine-man of some animal possessing keen sight was selected to accompany the war party. After the usual jugglery he sent his spirit animal away to determine the strength of the enemy, and quickly reached up his hand to receive it on its return, showing the people the medicine stone. So implicit was their faith in these sorcerers that the movements of the war party depended absolutely upon their predictions of success or failure. The same custom prevailed when preparing for important games between rival divisions of the tribe. The medicine-man who mistakenly prophesied success, and thereby caused the loss of much property to those who relied on his predictions, was usually in danger of being killed by the angry losers.

A peculiar belief of the Papago is one called *áâk*. If a bird, or almost any animal, especially the coyote, is encountered in one's path acting at all peculiarly, as fluttering the wings in the case of the bird, or sitting up and whining in the case of the coyote, it is regarded as an infallible sign of the approaching death of whomsoever one happens to be thinking of at that moment. An educated young Papago related the following story:

"One day I was ploughing my field, when a road-runner got in front of the plough. It seemed to be frightened, but instead of getting out of the way it simply ran along ahead of me. After a while I grew tired of seeing that bird always running in front of me, and threw a clod of earth at it. It fell over, kicked a few times, and before I came up to it, had died. That night when I went home I said, 'A strange thing happened to me to-day.' 'What was it?' asked my father. I began to tell, but had only mentioned the bird when he said, 'That is enough; stop right there!' The next day he asked whom I was thinking about when I saw the bird. I told him of my sister's little boy. His face became very sad. 'Father, what makes you so sad?' I asked. 'Why do you feel so bad?' Then he told me about *áâk*. From that time the family began to treat the little boy with the greatest kindness; he wanted nothing that he did not get. Nobody told him of what had happened, but from that day he began to grow thin and pale, and in less than three months he died."

Not a few of the religious observances of the Papago still persist even among those supposedly civilized, though they are kept from the knowledge of the whites. The maturity ceremony for girls is yet in favor, its whole purpose being to make the girl a strong, healthy, industrious, and virtuous woman. It consists of a four-nights' dance, beginning soon after darkness and lasting until daybreak, with a brief intermission at midnight. Two lines of dancers, men and women alternating, face each other, opposite dancers being of opposite sex, with a singer standing at the head of one line and the girl beside him. The dancing consists of a few steps, forward and back. The songs used are intended only for this occasion, and during the four nights none may be repeated. On the morning following the fourth night the girl bathes, and in the afternoon goes with her parents to see the medicine-man. Her parents stand on either side of her, while the medicine-man waves his eagle feathers over her to invoke divine blessing. Then he mixes a little clay with water and she drinks, thus ending the ceremony. To sleep during the four days would cause the girl to develop into a lazy woman; to eat food containing salt, or to touch meat or fire, would bring sickness upon the family.

One of the most striking of the old dances was the War Dance, culminating on the fourth night in the ceremony known as Tâtwóhlĭ, "We Tie." The Ghost Medicine-man held up a deerskin bag to catch the spirits of enemies killed in battle. The spirit of a man who had killed an Apache came rushing through the air, pursued by that of the slain Apache. The former was allowed to pass, while the latter was caught in the bag, which was quickly tied and passed over the Ghost Medicine-man's shoulders to four old men sitting behind. Thus the souls of many enemies were kept from entering the good land of the hereafter. If an inexperienced medicine-man were allowed to lead in this ceremony, he might become frightened and entrap the spirit of a tribesman, causing him to lose his reason in a few months. Hence men of high repute were always selected to conduct the War Dance.

SECTION SIX: Arts

Apsaroke (Crow)

ARTS

The handicraft of the Apsaroke was naturally seen at its best in clothing and articles of adornment. They were a proud people, rich in the things dear to wild tribes of the highlands, and the women lavished their best thoughts and labor on garments to beautify themselves in the eyes of the men, and still more on the clothing of their husbands in the desire that none should be more splendidly clad.

The nature of their life gave the Apsaroke a great deal of comparative leisure, and they delighted in fashioning fine garments from skins and in embroidering them in striking colors with porcupine-quills and beads. Nor were they satisfied with adorning themselves alone: their saddle-horses also were bedecked in gorgeous trappings. The saddles used by the women were made with a very high horn front and back, ornamented with beads or quills, and from each was suspended a large embroidered pendant. The stirrups, of bent willow, were covered with beaded skin. Just behind the saddle hung large decorated saddle-bags, so long that their fringes almost swept the ground, and an embroidered breast-piece was suspended from the horse's neck. The bridle was covered with beadwork, and a broad decorated piece extended from foretop halfway to the nose. An elaborate crupper was fastened to the saddle, and horses ridden by women were further equipped with a pair of finely made pouches, one on each side at the rear of the saddle.

Shields were made by men skilled in their fashioning. A piece of thick hide taken from the neck of an old buffalo bull was thoroughly dried in a slightly concave form, and cut in circular shape. It was then tested by shooting arrows at it, and if it was proof against them it was painted according to the desire of the owner, the design generally symbolizing some vision seen by him. Often the rawhide body was covered with deerskin and the design painted on this, and the whole enclosed in another casing of deerskin drawn together with a string at the back. Shields not in use were zealously cared for by the women, and were the very pride of their lives. Many of the shields became great medicine and passed from generation to generation.

Bows were made of elk-horn and sheep-horn and from cedar. The horn was boiled, straightened, worked into shape, and spliced to obtain the necessary length of about three and a half feet. Threads of sinew from the neck and shoulder of the buffalo were stretched on a flat piece of wood the width of the bow, and when this band was dry it was carefully taken from its temporary support and placed in the ground in order to moisten it and give it pliancy. This backing was then carefully fastened on the bow with strong glue, made by boiling the neck-skin of the elk, membrane from beaver-tails, tips of elk-horns, and hide scrapings.

Arrow-points were chipped from flint or carved from bone or horn. Lance-shafts were made of red birch, a little longer than the height of a man, and often were tipped with a prong of elk-horn.

As with other hunting tribes, domestic utensils were extremely simple. Kettles made of rawhide from the flank of the buffalo formed the usual cooking pots, the water being boiled by dropping in heated stones. This method was discovered by those "who had big hearts and were always looking for thoughts." Pots that held a couple of gallons were made of gray soapstone. A buffalo-paunch was used for carrying water, while the pericardium served as a smaller water-bag. Box-elder gnarls were fashioned into bowls, and horns of the mountain-sheep and buffalo into smaller dishes, cups, and spoons. Pottery cooking utensils were made to a limited extent, but they were too easily broken in travelling to be of great service.

In the old times at permanent camps tipi-shaped structures of logs and brush were set up for the women to cook in, and close by were pitched the dwelling tipis of skin. Before the acquisition of horses a lodge was made of eight to ten buffalo-skins, sometimes as few as five, and the slender poles were of the lightest kind of fir, as they had to be carried on the backs of the men and women.[1] In later times, as many as sixteen of the largest skins were required, while one who had seen a lodge in a vision made his dwelling of twenty hides; but to use more than eighteen would offend the spirits, unless one had received such a vision or bought the right from the man who had seen it.

The inner lining, which fitted closely to the ground, was the height of a tall man. Every year they put up new lodges, using the old covers for inner curtains, for leggings, moccasins, and other clothing. A large square of old tipi-covering was frequently used by a warrior as a saddle, as a shield from rain and wind, and, with a sort of draw-string around the edge, as a large bag in which food and clothing could be placed and kept dry when rivers were crossed.

Both the men and the women of the Apsaroke were better dressed than other tribes of the Northwest, for their mountain

---

[1] The Apsaroke never used the travois, either with dogs or with horses.

home-land furnished an abundance of the skins of bighorn sheep, deer, elk, and panther, in addition to the seemingly inexhaustible supply of buffalo-hides.

The dresses of the women were made usually of mountain-sheep skins; they were fringed on both sides and at the bottom, and were ornamented both front and back with a yoke of fringe. Down the sleeves and around the neck they were embroidered with porcupine-quills or beads, and from top to bottom dotted thickly with elk-teeth, while many others were fastened in the bottom fringe as bangles. The number of tusks on a dress depended, in a measure, on the wealth and standing of the family, an exceptionally fine garment requiring more than a thousand such ornaments. At the climax of the life of the Apsaroke a good horse purchased a hundred, and no self-respecting man presumed to marry unless he and his family could furnish the elk-teeth necessary to adorn a wife's dress.

Over the dress was worn a small, fine-haired buffalo-robe, well-tanned, and ornamented from the head to the tail with a broad stripe of quills or beads. At intervals along this band were circles of embroidery, and on each side other designs were placed. The leggings were usually of deerskin or mountain-sheep skin, made to fit snugly, extending from the ankle to above the knee, and on each, directly above the heel, was embroidered a large four-pointed star. Moccasins also were close-fitting, without stiff rawhide soles.

The women devoted a great deal of thought to dress and personal appearance, that the eyes of the men might be pleased. The hair was worn parted in the middle from front to back, hanging loosely over each shoulder, and tied at the end with a thong and an ornament, but not braided. Later, when they saw the Nez Percé women with their neatly braided hair, they adopted that custom. They used a porcupine-tail for a hairbrush and gave their locks great care, dressing them daily with a perfume of sweet-scented herbs and musk of the beaver.

The men wore deerskin shirts at all times when they were not about their own tipis. When the warrior had gained honors, they were indicated on the shirt that he wore on special occasions, each weasel-tail, scalp, lock of hair, or feather indicating some deed of bravery. The leggings were made usually of antelope-skin, with broad fringed flaps at the sides. Buffalo-robes from two- or three-year-old cows were worn with the hair inside, the head coming over the left shoulder, and a band of beadwork crossed the skin from side to side. Bear-claw necklaces were a favorite decoration, and strings of discs cut from the scapula of the buffalo and polished were often worn about the neck. In the old time they used no loin-cloth; indeed, as late as seventy-five years ago some of the old men had not yet adopted that article of dress.

One feature of the hairdressing was different from the custom of any neighboring tribe — that of wearing the hair in many long strands, similarly to the practice of the tribes in southwestern Arizona. The Apsaroke, moreover, greatly increased its natural length by working in other hair, so that sometimes the strands were so long as almost to touch the ground. Some of the men continued this fashion to within the last thirty years. On ceremonial occasions many of the young men imitated this manner of hairdressing by having many long locks fastened to a band worn at the back of the head. Both the real hair and the introduced strands were decorated from end to end with spots of red pigment.

SECTION SEVEN: Warfare

Nootka

WARFARE

The various groups of Nootka villages were mutually hostile.
Permanent peace and friendship existed only within the limits of
the dialectic unit, and not always then. Between these groups there
were intervals of peace for purposes of trade, the news of the truce
being spread by means of messengers sent among their nearest
neighbors from the villages that desired to be visited by trading
parties of other tribes. From these neighbors the report quickly
flew to the most distant parts of the west coast. In the absence of
such a truce any canoe passing the village of another tribe or encountered travelling was fair game for the fighting man who felt
impelled to enhance his reputation by taking a head or capturing a
slave. In spite of this condition there was considerable communica-
tion between the tribes; but travellers generally moved in large
parties, unless they were under the protection of a man allied by
birth to the tribe they were visiting.

When the head chief, whether on his own initiative or at the
request of a warrior desirous of glory or revenge, decided that an
expedition should be launched against a certain tribe, he called his
professional fighting men and revealed his purpose. They never
refused. On the following day he had his speaker assemble the
people and announce the plan. Any man without experience in
fighting, but desirous of becoming a warrior, might make a speech
declaring his intention to join the party. Then all the members of
the expedition disappeared for ceremonial purification. Although,
as a rule, he would not accompany them, the chief also bathed,
praying that his men might be successful and that no one of them
might be killed, and addressing such gods as Moon, Sun, and
Mountain Chief. In very important cases they bathed morning
and night during the waxing of ten moons, and of course they
practised continence. The war-party travelled only at night. Near
their destination they drew their canoes into the woods, purified
themselves again, and rubbed their individual medicine on their
bodies in order to make themselves invisible to the enemy. Meanwhile the scout canoe reconnoitred. After spending perhaps two
nights and two days in purification, they put their craft into the
water and moved by night toward the village. They landed and crept
cautiously toward the houses, holding hands in order that none
might stumble and give the alarm. In groups of two or three they
drew aside the mat doors and entered the houses that had been

assigned to them. Crouching in the darkness the marauders waited until they heard the signal, usually a screech-owl's hoot, of the party that had farthest to go, or until a scream announced that some one had been aroused. Then they fell upon their victims with spears, knives, and clubs, killing the men and capturing women and children. The entire population having been killed, captured, or scattered in flight, the invaders plundered the chests of food and clothing, fired the houses, and retreated to the canoes, which at the beginning of the attack had been brought into shallow water in front of the village.

During the absence of the warriors their women spent much time in singing, and Clayoquot women, in order to ensure the return of their men, would take two or three hairs at the temple and draw them slowly between their fingers. As soon as the returning canoes were seen, all the villagers dressed and marched to the beach, some striking batons on a sounding-board which they carried, and all singing. The severed heads of the enemy were set up on poles along the shore, or placed on prominent rocks, and the slaves were either claimed by the chief or left in the hands of their captors as a mark of his favor.

Sanguinary quarrels between individuals or factions were not infrequent. Murder for a price was a recognized custom, whether with a weapon, or by poison in the food of a guest, or by the supposedly occult practices of sorcerers.

Meares describes the departure and return of a war-party in August, 1788, in these words:

"Previous to our departure, we confirmed our friendship with Maquilla and Callicum [chiefs of the Mooachaht], with the usual interchange of presents. These chiefs had been for some time preparing for an hostile expedition against an enemy at a considerable distance to the Northward [probably either Quatsino or Kyuquot sound], and were now on the point of setting forward. Some of the nations in the vicinity of the Northern Archipelago [Queen Charlotte islands], had, it seems, invaded a village about twenty leagues to the Northward of King George's Sound [Nootka sound], under the jurisdiction, and which had been left to the particular government of his grandmother.[1]

---

[1] The father of Múqinna (Maquilla) had married the daughter of the head chief of the Ehatisaht. The aged woman who "ruled" the village occupied her place because she was the widow of the former chief, and not because she happened to be the grandmother of Múqinna, as Meares thought. It was only because there were no direct male heirs that she became the chief, and when she died, Kóhlanna, a younger brother of Múqinna, succeeded her.

"At this place the enemy had done considerable mischief, — murdering some of the people, and carrying others into captivity. On the arrival of a messenger at Nootka [Yuquot, principal village of the Mooachaht, at Friendly cove, Nootka sound] with the news of these hostilities, the inhabitants became instantly inflamed with a most active impatience for revenge; and nothing was thought of amongst them, but the means of gratifying it.

"We embraced this opportunity of binding the chiefs, if possible, unalterably to us, by furnishing them with some fire-arms and ammunition, which would give them a very decided advantage over their enemies. Indeed we felt it to be our interest that they should not be disturbed and interrupted by distant wars; and that, if necessity should compel them to battle, that they should return victorious. This unexpected acquisition of force animated them with new vigour; for they had already confessed that they were going to attack an enemy who was more powerful, numerous and savage than themselves.

"We attempted to instill into their minds the humanity of war, — and they had actually promised to punish the enemies they should take in battle with captivity, and not, as had been their general practice, with death. But it could not be supposed that the doctrines of our humane policy would be remembered by a savage nation burning with revenge, in the moment of battle; and we are sorry to add, that this expedition ended in a most shocking scene of blood and massacre.

"The power that Maquilla carried with him on this occasion, was of a formidable nature. His war canoes contained each thirty young, athletic men, and there were twenty of these vessels, which had been drawn from the different villages under the subjection of Maquilla. — Comekela had the command of two boats :—They moved off from the shore in solemn order, singing their song of war. The chiefs were cloathed in sea-otter skins; and the whole army had their faces and bodies painted with red ochre, and sprinkled with a shining sand [mica], which, particularly when the sun shone on them, produced a fierce and terrible appearance. While the women encouraged the warriors, in the patriotic language of the Spartan dames, — to return victorious, or to return no more.

"The battles, or rather the attacks of these savage tribes, are we believe inconceivably furious, and attended with the most shocking actions of barbarous ferocity. They do not carry on hostilities by regular conflicts; but their revenge is gratified, their sanguinary appetites quenched, or their laurels obtained by the operations of sudden enterprize and active strategem. . . .

"On the 27th, while we were visiting the village, Maquilla and Callicum returned from their war expedition; and, on entering the Sound, the little army gave the shout of victory. They certainly had obtained some advantages, as they brought home in their canoes several baskets, which they would not open in our presence, and were suspected by us, as it afterwards proved, by the confession of Callicum, to contain the heads of enemies whom they had slain in battle, to the amount of thirty; but this victory was not purchased without some loss on the side of the powers of Nootka.

"The chiefs now returned the arms they had received from us, but the ammunition was entirely expended : — we perceived, indeed, that the muskets had been fired several times; and Callicum assured us that they had taken ample vengeance for the hostilities exercised against them; and had, besides, made a great booty of sea-otter skins, in which they were all arrayed."

The pettiness of most of this primitive warfare may be illustrated by the following history of the encounters between the Makah and the Quilliute.

One summer a man at Warmhouse [a fishing village] invited the Quilliute, and only a few came. The following night some one killed three of them, a man and two women. When the other Quilliute learned of this, one of their young warriors led a party to Warmhouse and stabbed a chief in the back without killing him, and wounded another in the arm. In the ensuing struggle the Makah killed all the attacking party except one, who escaped by the help of certain Makah relatives. After hiding for some time in the woods, he went home along the beach and reported the news. The chief who was stabbed in the back subsequently died of the wound.

The next summer when the Makah were fishing at Warmhouse, they decided to make war on the Quilliute, and sent to Tatoosh, the other summer village, for help. Twenty canoes with crews of eight men armed with muzzle-loading guns and bows set out. The party stopped at Ozette to make their final plans. One of the bravest Ozette men wanted to go directly to James island, the refuge of the Quilliute, and as no other leader was willing to do so, he planned to go alone with his crew. Two of the chiefs said they would go up Quilliute river and watch for canoes, and the rest were to lie hidden near the island.

They reached their destination at night, and the canoes took up their positions. Soon those on the river saw a man and a woman coming downstream in a canoe, and the man, catching sight of the war-canoes, leaped overboard and escaped. The woman was captured. Later the two canoes went down the river again, and passing the island after daylight were shot at without damage. The proposed attack on the island had not been made, and the Quilliute taunted them with their failure. They now paddled away to the north toward home, but half way to Ozette, out of sight of the Quilliute, they landed, and scouts sent back along the shore saw their enemies preparing to fish. The Makah paddled toward the island, close along the shore and in single file. They were not detected until they were quite near the island, and so they succeeded in intercepting the unarmed fishermen and killing several.

The following summer the Makah heard that the Quilliute were coming for revenge, but it seemed that there was difficulty in organizing a party. Finally four brothers came overland and down Suez river. They stopped at Waatch creek. A man from Warmhouse, armed with a gun, happened along, and they gave chase, but he escaped across the creek. This man was Dahlúka, and he was a noted runner. The four brothers went home, and nothing more happened that summer.

A year later, in the autumn, the Ozette having returned to their home for the winter, a single Quilliute came to visit relatives. The chief immediately sent a messenger to invite the visitor to a feast, and hired a man to kill him. So the Quilliute was murdered. By this the Quilliute were greatly angered, and three years later Sítadu, a squat, vicious man, selected four companions and came to Ozette. They lay in wait south of the village, and before daybreak they saw a man pass them, looking for sea-food cast ashore. They did not molest him. It grew light, and another man passed, unarmed. They called to him, and he recognized Sítadu as a relative of his. Sítadu told him to sit down, and asked why and how the Quilliute man had been murdered three years previously. The man refused to speak of it, and asked to be released, as he was on his way to work at a canoe. When they still insisted, he said he would go back immediately to Ozette. He stood up, but the four men held him, and Sítadu, exasperated, exclaimed, "Are you going back at once?" With that he stabbed his relative four times, and the man fell to the ground. They killed him, and hid the body among the bushes.

A woman approached, and two of them stabbed her to death and left the corpse on the beach. Soon they heard a man chopping wood, and creeping up slowly they saw the workman, and a little girl seated on a log and cleaning sea-weed. She saw the bushes move, and told the man, but he paid no attention. She sat there and watched for further signs. At this time a woman passed on down the beach. Then Sítadu shot the man in the thigh, and he fell between two logs. Another Quilliute sprang upon the log and shot him in the side, but the wound was shallow. They seized the girl, ran southward along the shore, and overtook the woman. She proved to be an aunt of Sítadu, and he reassured her and went on. They came to a large stump on the beach, and found the man who had first passed them early in the morning. He drew a knife, ready to fight. The others, recognizing him also as a relative of Sítadu, grounded their guns, but he was suspicious. They told him to go home, but he was afraid to turn his back and would not move until they went on. Meanwhile the woman had hurried to the village and told of the two men killed and the little girl taken.

The first man killed had a kinsman among the Quilliute, and one of them was very angry because the relatives of Sítadu had been spared but his own killed. In the winter of the same year he asked his brother and two others to go with him to Ozette and remedy this inequality. When they reached the hiding place used by Sítadu, they waited to see if their man would come along the beach again. And early in the morning he came. One of them shot, and he ran toward the water, wounded. Another fired and killed him. A wood-chopper ran to the village and reported that he had heard shots.

Meanwhile another Ozette came along the beach, and finding a gun-cover he looked carefully about and saw the tracks of four men hurrying southward. He knew they were made by Quilliute, and he quickly carried the news to the village. The warriors armed themselves and started out, and at the place where the shooting had occurred one of them saw a bit of rag fluttering in the breeze. Thus they found the dead man. They perceived the Quilliute, but soon abandoned the chase.

Late in the fall of the following year, when there was snow on the ground, four other Quilliute came north. They lay in wait near the village, and at dawn they killed two women without betraying their presence. Two old women gathering fuel near a brook saw a woman's foot projecting from behind a stump, and then, discovering the body, they turned and ran. Two of the Quilliute gave chase, and shot one of them dead and broke the arm of the other. They caught the wounded one but soon released her, and she ran to the village. Then the men rushed out, and while some recovered the bodies for burial, others followed the enemy. From the point the six pursuers saw four men on the long beach, and at the next point they overtook one of them. The other Quilliute had taken his gun and ammunition, but the Makah did not know this, and were afraid to follow when he plunged into the forest. At the third point they gave up the pursuit, the Quilliute having taken to the woods.

Two years later a Quilliute came to Ozette to make peace. He had many relatives there, and having taken no part in the hostilities he was safe. He went to the home of his nearest relative and said that Sítadu was the only Quilliute who desired to continue the war, and declared that he would bring this man to Ozette and offer peace. The next day he returned home, and it was not long before he had persuaded Sítadu to accompany him and four others to Ozette. It was agreed that the messenger was to lodge with his relatives, and that Klíklîhahlîk ("face painted red") was to invite the others and kill Sítadu. So this man gave Sítadu a seat at the end of the row, where his wife was preparing the meal. His knife was hidden under his wife's dress, and he himself sat between her and the warrior. When they began to eat, he noticed that Sítadu had a knife partly concealed by his blanket, and he asked to see it, saying: "You ought to trust me. I would not carry a knife if I visited you." The other Quilliute had guns within reach. At the end of the meal the host gave Sítadu the usual bunch of shredded cedar-bark, and when his guest shut his eyes in wiping his face, he grasped him by the hair, drew his head back, and stabbed him in the neck with the man's own knife. The door opened and some villagers came in, and the Quilliute, with guns ready, backed to the wall. But the intermediary explained to the Makah that their last enemy had been killed, and that these others were friendly. So the Quilliute were permitted to return to their homes, and there they explained to the family of Sítadu that he had been killed in a mêlée from which they had luckily escaped. There was no further trouble between the two tribes.

Village feuds could be as venomous and futile as some of these almost puerile wars. A Makah feud was carried on in the following manner:

The daughter of the whaler Waáli and a sister of the warrior Káshid quarrelled, and such epithets were exchanged that the two men felt themselves involved. Káshid threatened to stab Waáli. There was much talk among the people, and some said that the two had agreed to fight it out on the beach. For four years nothing happened, but Káshid nursed his wrath. One morning when as usual the men sat talking on the platform above the beach, the husband of Káshid's sister surreptitiously placed his foot on Waáli's blanket. Káshid went up the terrace, crept unseen toward the platform, rushed upon his enemy, and grasped his hair. The foot on his blanket prevented Waáli from rising further than his hands and knees, and Káshid struck a glancing blow at his waist. He released his hold, and Waáli stood up almost unhurt. His sons rushed to his aid, but the crowd prevented further trouble, and the chief, who now appeared on the scene, commanded peace.

For four days each constantly expected an attack, and other men stayed indoors as much as possible. The tension however was gradually relieved. Two years later Káshid was heard to say that he would some day shoot his enemy, and the sons of Waáli saw no way but to arrange a battle. At the end of the third year a date was fixed. Early in the morning Waáli, his four sons, and two slaves painted their faces and bodies black, with black stripes on their legs, and each wound a blanket around the left arm, letting a portion of it hang. All had guns except one slave. They went to the shore, the eldest son leading, and stood in a line across the beach. After a while came Káshid with four guns. His face was black and his body red. He was stripped except for a belt, which held two of the guns. He ran rapidly down the beach to a canoe and crouched behind it. A slave joined him, and a relative took a position behind a whale's shoulderblade. Waáli's party advanced. Káshid leaped upon the canoe and fired at the one nearest the water, and the bullet struck the sand. He ran to the other end of the canoe and shot at the next man, but without effect. Then he fired the other two guns at them, grasped the four weapons, and ran to his house, pursued by Waáli and his men, who shot as they ran. At the door a bullet glanced from his gun-stock and struck his thigh, causing him to fall. Some one opened the door, and he staggered in. Meanwhile the two slaves had been exchanging arrows. Waáli had not yet used the charge in his gun. He now went to the house and stood near the door with his back inadvertently against a loophole. Káshid, having reloaded his guns, perceived that some one was leaning against one of his loopholes, and thinking that it must be one of his enemies, he cocked a gun and pulled the trigger. It missed fire, and Waáli, suddenly aware of his danger, ran away.

That night no one stirred. The next day it was reported that Káshid was suffering from his wound and was not expected to live long. A day later he sent a relative for a medicine-man to remove the bullet, and bribed him to report that he could not long survive. In fact the wound was only a trifle. In the afternoon the people heard a war-cry, and on rushing out they beheld Káshid with a gun in each hand, and painted with white, red, and black stripes from head to foot like his guardian spirit. He walked up and down the beach, challenging his enemies, but no one appeared. At dusk he went to the house of Waáli and shot into it, but struck no one.

The sons of Waáli felt that they had not enough guns, and before dawn the next day the family started for Quilliute, where they traded their sister for four guns. Then they returned, and none knew what they had done. In their absence however Káshid had gone in a canoe to Baada to have his wound treated, and when he returned he did not propose a fight. He sickened, and a few years later in an epidemic of smallpox he killed himself with a knife.

A Clayoquot war-song runs thus:

> I am not afraid, I am not afraid!
> If I take out a war-canoe, I am not afraid!
> Why are you afraid? I am not afraid!

SECTION EIGHT: Social Customs

Tiwa: Kivas and Societies

KIVAS AND SOCIETIES

On the south side of the stream there are four subterranean kivas (*ṭûaṭánă*, from *ṭûnă*, house), three of which are outside the pueblo wall:

1. Pâ-ṭáï-ṭûaṭánă, Water People Kiva
2. Fĭă-ṭáï-ṭûaṭánă, Feather People Kiva
3. Ḳwa-ḥláo-ṭûaṭánă, Ax Big Kiva

The fourth south-side kiva was unnamed by the present informant, who professed to have forgotten the name. It is kept in repair, he said, as a memorial of ancient times when it was used. Few people know what society used it, and no meetings have been held in it for many generations. None of these statements is credited by the writer. Keeping an unused building in repair for sentimental reasons is something entirely alien to Indian practice, and the informant's efforts to remember the name of the kiva were too elaborate to be genuine. Undoubtedly this kiva is the scene of rituals so important and so sacred that he did not dare risk being questioned about them. On the north side are three of these ceremonial chambers:

4. Fíalo-ḥla-ṭáï-ṭûaṭánă, Seashell Big [that is, abalone] People Kiva
5. Chĭă-ṭáï-ṭûaṭánă, Flint People Kiva
6. Ṭû-ṭáï-ṭûaṭánă, Day People Kiva

The kivas are named for the ceremonial groups that respectively meet in them. These societies, with their subdivisions or associated orders, are as follow, extinct orders being indicated by the asterisk, and kiva affiliation by numerals:

1. Pâ-ṭáïna^n, Water People
   1a. Ḳâ^n-ṭáïna^n, Corncob People
   1b. Fâ^n-ṭáïna^n, Snow People
   1c. Iăkâ^n-ṭáïna^n, Hail People
2. Fĭă-ṭáïna^n, Feather People
   2a. Ṭálo-ṭáïna^n, Parrot People
   2b. Ṭo-ṫŝólumu^n-ṭáïna^n, Bird Yellow [that is, summer warbler] People
3. Ḳwa-ḥláo-ṭáïna^n, Ax Big People
   3a. Ḥúfo^n-ḳwaḥláo-ṭáïna^n, Sweet-corn-meal Ax-big People
4. Fíalo-ḥla-ṭáïna^n, Seashell Big People
   4a. Fâ^n-ṭáïna^n, Snow People
   4b. Iăkâ^n-ṭáïna^n, Hail People
   4c. Fĭă-ṭáï-ḳwaḥláo-ṭáïna^n, Feather People Ax-big People
   4d. Iă-ṭáïna^n, Corn People
5. Chĭă-ṭáïna^n, Flint People
   5a. Pá-ḥlul-ṭáïna^n, Water Drip [that is, dew] People

6. Ṭû-ṭáïna^n, Day People
   6a. Há^{n}l-ṭáïna^n, Shell People
   6b. Tól-tû-ṭáïna^n, Sun House People
   6c. Ṭû-ṭáïna^n, House People
   6d. Pĭă-pâtû-ṭáïna^n, Mountain White People
* Ḳáki-ṭáïna^n, Crow People
* Ṭohwă-ṭáïna^n, Fox-coyote People
* Chiw-ṭáïna^n, Eagle People
* Ḳwaĭă-ṭáïna^n, Magpie People
* Kâl-ṭáïna^n, Wolf People
* Kúa-ṭáïna^n, Bear People
* Pách!ă-ṭáïna^n, Ice People
* Iă-ṫŝolu-ṭáïna^n, Corn Yellow People
* Iă-ch!áluna-ṭáïna^n, Corn Blue People
* Iă-pátûna-ṭáïna^n, Corn White People
* Ûḥlaíto-ṭáïna^n, Green-leaf People
* Pâchunó-ṭáïna^n, Shell-bead People

These groups have been regarded as clans, which appears to be an erroneous conception. (1) A male child at birth is dedicated to any one of these groups, and not necessarily to that of his father. (2) The groups are definitely associated with certain kivas, and nowhere do clans sustain such a relation to the ceremonial chambers. (3) The informant was positive in his declaration that he would have the right to marry any woman not actually related to him, and was frankly puzzled by the investigator's explanation of the clan concept, being plainly quite ignorant of the system.

On the other hand it is to be noted that the names of three of the six principal groups, most of the associated groups, and all of the extinct ones, are such as the Pueblo Indians commonly apply to their clans. Moreover, the origin legend relates that they travelled in divisions corresponding to these groups. Again, there is the statement of Coronado's chronicler, quoted heretofore: "It has 18 divisions; each one has a situation as if for two ground plots." Just what this means is not clear, but it points to the former existence of clans with separate land holdings. The fact that the extinct groups named above, added to the six existent principal societies, total eighteen, may or may not be coincidence.

Inspection of the list of names given above reveals in some instances a logical connection between the principal, or type, group and the subdivisions associated with it. Feather naturally includes Parrot and Summer Warbler. Water suggests Snow and Hail, and conceivably Corncob, since the production of corn depends on water. Shell, a shining object, is logically associated with White Mountain and Sun House, and the addition of House may have been suggested by Sun House. With respect to the others the case is more difficult. Big Ax and Sweet Cornmeal certainly have little in common, and Flint and Dripping Water are equally puzzling. Big Seashell connotes water, hence Snow, Hail, and Corn, almost the same trio found associated with Water, but in addition there is Feather Big-ax, which apparently was originally made up of individuals from the type groups of kivas number two (Feather) and three (Big Ax).

Snow and Hail are named as separate groups, yet they are under the leadership of one man. One group bearing these names is associated with Feather kiva on the south side, another with Big Seashell kiva on the north side. Feather Big-Ax and Corn, associated with Big Seashell kiva, are similarly paired under one leader. In this kiva there are from fifteen to twenty men, seven of whom are Snow-Hail.

At birth every male child is dedicated by his parents to one of these groups, which is not necessarily that to which his father belongs. Some female children are similarly dedicated, and their duties will be to keep the kiva in repair and in order. They will take no part in the ceremonies. The work of cleaning and repairing the kivas however is not limited to these female lay-members, for the men may summon their wives or female relatives to do it, even if they be not "members."

In each kiva the head-man belongs to the name-group, not to one of the subdivisions. The head of Big Seashell is the North cacique, Fíãlohla-ṭáïnă ("big-seashell person"), which is also the title of any member of the society; and the head of Water is the South cacique, Pâ-ṭáïnă ("water person"). Each cacique secretly trains a successor, preferably his son. But if his son is not fitted for the position, he selects some other of his own type-group. The general membership knows nothing of this man's identity, which however the cacique reveals to one person, so that in case of his sudden death the man in training may have a witness to the fact that he has been designated for the position.

In 1924 two young boys were removed from school for instruction in Big Ax kiva.[1] They are commonly said to be under training

[1] The boys were taken from school about the month of March, professedly for "training by the cacique." In May the governor, who had been threatened with arrest for this contravention of regulations, issued a call to all the Pueblos for a council at San Felipe. A San Felipe member of this council related to a Santo Domingo informant of the writer what there occurred. The Taos delegate, he said, called to their attention that all the Indians knew the Taos custom, and all must stand together in opposition to the authorities and in support of the native rites, and particularly all were to refuse information respecting the Indian religion and customs. The San Felipe man explained to his Santo Domingo friend that in every year a boy and a girl were taken from Taos to the lake from which the Pueblo Indians emerged upon the earth (in southern Colorado), and there were drowned in order to prevent the recurrence of a legendary deluge. The Taos delegate, he said, did not refer to this custom in plain words, but everybody understood what he meant.

If all this be true it seems likely that the Taos head-men intend to sacrifice one of the two boys along with a young girl, and later to send the other boy back to school as an evidence of their fidelity to a pledge made to the authorities; the missing one, of course, to be reported dead by natural causes.

The writer (and previous volumes of this series would seem to exonerate him of the charge of easy credulity) believes that these quadrennial sacrifices still persist. The sacrifice of a boy and a girl is a not uncommon incident in Pueblo mythology, and mythologic events are largely a reflection of actual practice. History records few instances of adherence to ancient customs in the face of an opposing civilization equal to that displayed by the Pueblo Indians; and while the idea of human sacrifice within the borders of the United States is so unlooked for as to appear ridiculous, it is in fact no more than should be expected in view of the known prevalence of the custom in Mexico a few centuries ago. It is really not much more savage than the self-inflicted tortures of the New Mexican penitentes, a sect which grows more flourishing from year to year.

fourteen months, but as a matter of fact their instruction occupies only the first thirty days, after which they are "thinking of what they have been taught." They spend their days with other boys playing outside the village and roaming through the woods. They may not play inside the pueblo walls. Returning, they go at once to the kiva and spend the night there under the care of a member appointed by the kiva chief. But during the thirty days of instruction all members are present and sleep there.

At such times the Snow-Hail division is not permitted to be present, for the reason that its members are men who have not "started from the roots," that is, they have not as boys undergone this instruction and do not belong to the type-group of the kiva. Therefore the matters of instruction are kept secret from them. They take part however in the other activities of the society. The leader of Snow-Hail has been overwhelmed with offers of youths for membership, because of the fact that many boys, lacking instruction in the kiva by reason of attendance at school, wish to join his group, in which preliminary training is not required. But he holds to the view that membership shall be limited to a reasonable number. Therefore at the present time there are many young men who have no part in the ceremonial system. They are forced, however, to participate in dances, under pain of the imposition of a small fine and the frowns of the elders.

In midsummer Water Person, that is, the South cacique, having carefully observed the rising of the sun with reference to landmarks in the skyline of the mountain range, and aware that it has reached its northern limit, summons his members to Water kiva. He announces the purpose, and four days later they meet in the cañon about half a mile from the pueblo, where they sing for rain and good crops. This is repeated on the fourth day following, and the next six days they spend, at least in part, at a different clearing in the cañon, carefully cleaning this dance-ground and building a booth of evergreens adorned with flowers. On the seventh morning they erect their altar in the booth, and in the presence of all the people, including women and children, they sing and pray.

The Water society having finished its summer solstice work, its leader visits some other kiva, any one he may happen to choose, to urge its members to do their part; and they do exactly what the Water People have just completed. Thus each ceremonial group performs, the entire cycle being concluded about the end of September.

This ceremonial use of the cañon is the reason visitors are strictly forbidden to enter the gorge without permission of the governor.

About the end of August and in September, some of these meetings in the cañon, where the altar is arranged in a booth, are followed in the afternoon by dancing by men and women dressed in their best clothing but not wearing special costumes. This dancing is said to be for pleasure.

At the winter solstice, Fân-ṭaïnă, or Iăkán-ṭaïnă, the head of the Snow-Hail division of Big Seashell kiva, summons his own men and all other members of the kiva, and sets up his altar. This occupies one evening, and he then goes to the leader of the Snow-Hail group of the Water People, who calls his kiva members together and does the same things.

The spirits supplicated for rain, snow, and hail are Hlăf̆sínan (singular, Hlăf̆sínă, the Taos equivalent of Kaf̆sína), who dwell in all springs and lakes. They are said not to be represented by masked personators. The head of the Snow-Hail group has possession of certain sacred objects, the nature of which will not be divulged but which are described as the "tools of the Hlăf̆sínan."

The Chífunănan (singular, Chí-funănă, "eye black-that") of Taos correspond to the Ḳú'sari of the Keres Indians. They paint in the same fashion as the Keres clowns: white body with black horizontal stripes, and black ovals about the eyes and mouth. They have the Ḳú'sari corn-husk ribbons, but instead of arranging the hair in the form of a curving horn they wear deerskin caps of similar shape. They probably compose a society, although as to that nothing is known. The Mexicans, and after them the local Americans, call them "chifonetti," an adaptation of the native term, which itself is equivalent to Isleta Shifunín (singular, Shífunídĕ), the name of one of the two ceremonial moieties of the southern pueblo.

There are, it is said, no societies of shamans for the curing of disease. The individual medicine-man is called ṭúină. He sings, sucks, and brushes the part with eagle-feathers and waves them about, charging them to declare the sorcerer that has caused the trouble. His pay is a sack or two of grain, a blanket or a deerskin, a horse or a cow. He attends on four successive nights, and is assisted by any ordinary men who are good singers and whom he pays.

APPENDIX ONE: Biographical Sketches

Brulé: Little Dog
Assiniboin: Long Fox
Assiniboin: Mosquito-Hawk
Ogalala: Red Cloud

Little Dog, *Shų"ka-la*

Brulé. Born 1848. First war-party at sixteen against the troops at the head of Platte
iver; horses were captured without fighting. The next year he led a party against a detach-
nent on Lodgepole creek; one soldier was killed and some horses were taken. Counted three
oups, one of the first grade, each while acting as war-leader, and was thrice wounded. Sorrow-
ng at the death of a sister, he went alone against the Pawnee, and nearing their camp gave
hase to a solitary hunter, but abandoned the pursuit because there was no one to testify that
e counted coup even if he had done so. That night he stole into the camp and captured five
orses. Participated in forty-one fights and fifteen horse-raids. Scouted for General Crook.

Long Fox, *Tokána-há"ska*

Assiniboin. Born in 1827 near Fort Berthold, North Dakota. He joined a war-party
gainst the Mandan, capturing three horses. On another expedition against the same people
e received an arrow wound. Subsequently, in an attack on the Assiniboin by the Sioux, he
illed one, and in another fight with them he counted a first coup. The Assiniboin met a
ar-party of Piegan, and he captured one. Long Fox led against the Sioux a war-party that
aptured seven horses. He never had a vision. He married at thirty.

Mosquito-hawk, *Susbécha*

Assiniboin. Born on the Missouri below Williston, North Dakota. When he was fourteen
e followed a war-party, but gained no honors. On his next four expeditions he had as little
uccess, but on the next he killed a Sioux. He fought against the Piegan, killing two, taking
scalp and counting a first coup. In another battle with the Piegan he killed one, counted
oup, and took a scalp. He never fasted, and never has had a vision. He married at seventeen.

Red Cloud, *Mahpíya-lúta* ("Scarlet Cloud")

Ogalala. Born 1822. At the age of fifteen he accompanied a war-party which killed eighty
Pawnee. He took two scalps and shot one man. At seventeen he led a party that killed eight
f the same tribe. During his career he killed two Shoshoni and ten Apsaroke. Once going
gainst the Apsaroke, he left the party and approached the camp on foot. About daylight a
nan came driving his herd to the range. Red Cloud charged him, killed him with arrows,
tabbed him with the Apsaroke's own knife, and scalped him; he then took his clothes and
tarted back, driving the horses. Men from the camp pursued, and a severe fight followed
etween the two parties. Once an Apsaroke captured his herd. He followed all night, and at
aylight caught up with and killed the raider. Red Cloud received his name, in recognition of
is bravery, from his father after the latter's death. Before that his name had been Two Arrows,
Ma"-nó"pa. His brother-in-law, *Nachíli*, gave him medicine tied up in a little deerskin bag.
Always before going to war Red Cloud rubbed this over his body. All the tribe regarded his
nedicine as very potent. He first gained notice as a leader by his success at Fort Phil. Kearny
n 1866, when he killed Captain Fetterman and eighty soldiers. In the following year he led a
arge party, two to three thousand, it is said, in an attack on a wood-train at the same post, but
vas repulsed with great loss. (See pages 37–39.) Previously only chief of the Bad Face band
f Ogalala, he became head-chief of the tribe after the abandonment of Fort Phil. Kearny.
Red Cloud was prevented from joining in the Custer fight by the action of General Mackenzie
n disarming him and his camp.

APPENDIX TWO: Note on the Indian Music

by Henry F. Gilbert

NOTE ON THE INDIAN MUSIC

In the course of my work in transcribing Indian melodies from phonographic cylinders for Volumes VI, VII, and VIII, one of the first things to impress me was the impossibility of representing these melodies accurately by means of our ordinary musical notation. The principal reason for this difficulty is that while our notation provides for the representation of certain definite degrees of pitch (and those only), the Indian habitually sings degrees of pitch for which we have no symbols. For instance, we can represent e (330 vibrations per second) and f (352 vibrations per second), but when the Indian sings a tone lying somewhere between these two (say 335 vibrations per second), our notation is powerless to represent this tone with accuracy.

In such cases I have written that note which most nearly approximated the tone sung by the Indian. A notation could easily have been invented which would have permitted the more accurate expression of Indian melody, but this would have been of questionable value. If the Indian deliberately uses a different scheme of tones and intervals from that of the civilized races, as has been suggested, one would naturally expect this difference to stand out clearly, or at least noticeably, in the course of several repetitions of the same song. But in the examination of more than sixty songs much variation appears in the repetitions of each one. As a general rule the repetitions fail to agree in length, rhythm, or accuracy of intonation; frequently they agree only in general contour. It can truthfully be said that in the case of the phonographic records examined by me for these three volumes no song is ever repeated twice exactly alike. Any single tone is liable to vary up or down at least a quarter of a tone, and in some cases the variation is as much as a full tone. It is more than likely that the Indian is somewhat blindly groping for the diatonic intervals which form the basis of civilized music, and that his deviations therefrom are not caused by a conscious disregard of them so much as by his inability to intone them accurately. In many instances, however, he is quite successful in his use of the usual diatonic intervals, and while he very rarely uses the complete diatonic scale, he frequently uses five or even six of the tones composing it.

But there is a great difference in his manner of using these tones from that of the civilized man. In the melody of civilized man the tones are all related to a central tone called the tonic or key-note, and however widely they may wander from this key-note, a definite relationship to it is always preserved, the melody usually ending upon the key-note itself. This relationship among the tones of a melody produces a definite musical atmosphere called a tonality or key. Among the Indians this sense of tonality is largely lacking. In the majority of songs no key is established which lasts throughout the song. Here and there a few measures definitely indicate a particular key, but the sense of this key is usually lost before the song ends. In many of the songs no key whatever, as we understand it, is established, such songs being more or less rhythmic yells upon certain tones, and sounding much as if they were intended for incantations rather than songs. An occasional song is found, however, in which the sense of tonality is quite perfect.

Although rhythm is of great importance to the Indian, it is my belief that he has not consciously developed any very complicated rhythmic schemes. All the rhythmic schemes which have come under my observation seem to be very simple, and the complexities which have arisen seem to me to have been purely accidental. When a song is accompanied by a drum-beat, it usually happens that the drummer keeps time in the most rigid and inflexible manner throughout the song. The singer, on the contrary, will introduce retards, accelerandos, pauses of different length, and numerous variations of time. There consequently arise many complicated rhythmic relations between the drum-beat and the melody. But inasmuch as both singer and drummer start with evident agreement as regards time and accent, it is quite probable that the subsequent complications are accidental rather than intentional.

The Indian's manner of singing has much to do with the peculiar character of his music. Embellishments such as grace-notes, trills, and shakes abound. Pure sustained tones are somewhat rare. Most long tones are broken up by a kind of fluttering or pulsing of the voice. In most instances this has been carefully indicated in the transcriptions. The Indian is also addicted to an exaggerated use of portamento, or the slurring of one tone into another. Instead of singing one definite tone after another he is very apt to glide from one tone to the next, producing the impression that he is feeling his way among the intervals. This has been indicated in the most marked cases by the sign $\searrow$ and in other cases, where it is not so apparent, by the slur $\frown$. Extended slurs have also been used to indicate phrasing, as is the custom in civilized music.

The Indian singer also takes many liberties with the time. Although rhythmic values are fairly well preserved, he introduces ritards and accelerandos, and sometime a long ritenuto, causing the end of a song to be sung at a much slower rate than the beginning. On the other hand songs that accompany dancing or other regular rhythmic movements are sung in strict time.

It is impossible, especially while listening to those Indian melodies of which the tonality is more or less perfect, to escape the conviction that the primitive music has been considerably influenced by the Indian's contact with the white man. In Nature melody is represented by the songs of birds, the sighing of the wind in the forest, the babbling of mountain brooks, and there is no doubt that the Indian in his first attempts at melody making was largely influenced by such sounds. Songs such as Wind in the Pines (Volume VII, page 94) and the Pelican Medicine-song (Volume VII, page 84) bear eloquent witness to his tendency to imitate natural sounds. But with the coming of white men a new musical element was brought to him: the element of tonality. Tonality is present in even the simplest folk-song sung by the rudest pioneer, and it is but natural that the Indian should imitate the song of the pioneers just as he had imitated the sounds of Nature. It is well known with what patience and perseverance the early Jesuit missionaries taught the Indians to sing church hymns, and when one listens to such songs as that on page 74 of Volume VIII, it seems certain that the Indian music of the present day shows this influence.

By no means the least interesting feature of an Indian song is the yell which precedes so many of them. This yell is usually a very complicated affair, and besides mere shouting is apt to consist of trills, shakes, slurs, and frequently short but quite well-defined musical phrases. When a muscial phrase is hinted at in a yell, the same phrase is usually to be found in a much more developed form in the subsequent song. This is to be expected, as the yell is simply a wild prelude to the song, a tuning up of the voice, the singer getting himself into the mood, as it were. Of course the yells practically defy accurate expression in musical notation. At first hearing they sound decidedly more akin to noise than to music. The voice glides with such rapidity and in such a slurring and sliding manner through so many changes of pitch that often only the approximate contour or melodic outline of the yell can be indicated. I nevertheless consider these yells to be more interesting, and certainly more significant from an ethnological point of view, than many of the melodies themselves.

Songs are frequently followed by yells, but these are not musically important, as they consist for the greater part of one or two shouts with a falling inflexion of the voice, and have no relation to the foregoing song. Sometimes, however, as in the Pelican Medicine-song (Volume VII, page 84), the yell at the end consists of long and beautifully sustained tones at the top of the voice.

Transcribing Indian melodies in ordinary musical notation is somewhat like forcing a square peg into a round hole: it can be accomplished by dint of sufficient exertion, but the original form will have suffered. The vital part of these melodies can be expressed in our notation, but many a delicate nuance of wild and wayward beauty will have disappeared. However, though the latter may be bruised in the process, enough of the spirit survives to make the transcription valuable, not only to the reader of to-day, but especially to the student of the future, who will find in such records as these his only opportunity to study this phase of primitive culture. It is in the songs of a people that we rightly look for the greatest spontaneity of self-expression.

HENRY F. GILBERT

APPENDIX THREE: Vocabulary

Western Algonquian Comparative Vocabulary

WESTERN ALGONQUIAN COMPARATIVE VOCABULARY

ANATOMICAL TERMS

English	Piegan	Cheyenne	Arapaho
ankle-joint	áħ-ko-kĭ-nak	vé-he-o-ó	wŭ-ná-i
arm	oħ-fŝí-mĭ-na^n	má-ahfŝ	bĕ-nĕs
blood	a-á-pŭn	má-e	bĕ-ŭ
bone	oħ-kín	hé-ku	hí-ḵu
chest	o-kín	hé-śhe-eo	há-kŭ-băt
chin	oħp-skí-nai	he-stó	wa-tá-kŭ-ŭ
ear	oħ-tó-kĭs	mah-to-vó-hfŝ	wá-na-tá-nŭ-ŭ
elbow-joint	oħ-kíns-fŝĭs	mah-fŝé-o	bĕ-tĭs
eye	o-wápsp	má-eħ	bĕ-sí-i-sĕ-ŭ
face	mos-tók-sís		wa-tá-ŭ-kbé-ŭ
finger	mo-kí-fŝĭs	mó-oeħ-ku	bă-ă-chĕ-tĭ-na
finger-nail	a-o-tán-o-kĭ-fŝĭs (finger shield)	hó-hóev	
foot	oħ-kŭfŝ	hé-hes	wá-aŧh
hair	o-kú-yes	mí-hi-vat	bé-i-ŧhă-ă
hand	o-fŝĭs	hmaí-eo	sé-i-ŧhă-ŧha
head	o-to-kán	má-ku	
heart	ós-tă-fŝĭp	hés-ta	bé-tă-ă^n
knee	o-tok-sís	hen-stán	chă-i-tă-yé-nĭħ
leg	o-wáp-i-săk	hma-fŝé-ku	wa-á-taħ
lip	o-tó-nĭs	mahfŝ	bĕs-sŭ-si
lungs	oħ-písfŝ	he'-pó-nfŝ	hí-i-ḵa-nŭ
mouth	ma-ó-yi	mahfŝ	bĕ-ti
neck	oħ-ko-kín	hé-uhfŝ	bĕ-tă-ní-wa
nose	oħ-ksĭ-sís	ma-év	bé-is
nostril	mó-pi-ki-nan	hma-tá-fŝom	bĕ-tă-ní-wa
toe	nĭk-śhú-o-kí-fŝĭs (below finger)	mó-oeħ-ku	bĕ-să-ă-no
toe-nail	a-o-tán-o-kĭ-fŝĭs	hó-hóev	bĕ-să-ă-ni-wa-ŭ
tongue	ma-fŝĭ-ní	vé-ta-nov	he-ní-i-ŧhan
tooth	pí-kĭn	vé-es	bé-i-chĭŧh

ANIMALS

antelope*	sâ-ki-ó-wa-ka-si	vó-ka-e	nĭ-sí-cha
badger*	mí-sĭn-skyu	ma-há-ka-e	
bat	mó-tu-in-sta-mi	mo-sés-ka-ne-chén-no-ve-na	wa-ŧhén-ŧha-né-hi
bear, black*	sík-ku-kyai-yu (black grizzly-bear)	mo-o-fŝe-náh-ko (black grizzly-bear)	
bear, grizzly-*	kyaí-yu	náh-ko	wŭħ
beaver*	ksís-ksta-ki (gnawer)	hó-ma-e	hă-băs
buffalo*	i-ní-wa		hi-ŧhé-i-nan
buffalo bull*	i-stá-mik	hó-to-a	
buffalo cow*	skín-ni-wa	meh	
buzzard	pi-ku-ḵí	ó-é	hă-chŭ-sŭ-hu

The names of animals used as food are indicated by stars.

English	Piegan	Cheyenne	Arapaho
coyote	ksĭ-ná-o	ó'-kohm	ḳa-á-hŭ-wŭ
crane*	sí-kam		tá-tha
crow	mai-stó	ó-kohch	wá-ḳŭch
curlew*	ma-kí-e-ni-ma		
deer, black-tail*	ís-sĭ-ko-tu-yi (blackish tail)	vá-u-tŝév	bí-hĭ-ı
deer, white-tail*	á-wa-tu-yi (tail flicker)		
dog*	i-mi-tá		
duck*	mi-ŭk-si-ká-tŝi		sí-i-sich
eagle, bald	tŝĭk-kĭ-kyí-ni	vó-a-ħá-e	
eagle, golden	pí-tô	netŝ	ni-é-hi-i
elk*	pụn-nu-ká	mó-e	
fish*	ma-míw	nó-ma-hne	ná-wa-ŭ
fox	iĕ-ku-tŝí-sí-no-pa (red kit-fox)	má-a-hó-he	bắ-ă-ko-u
fox, kit-	si-no-pá		
goose*	sa-aíw		né-i
gopher*	ó-maħ-ku-ka-ta	no-é-o	no-chí-i-tá-ťhe-i
grouse*	kĭtŝ-sí-tŝĭm		ché-ta-i-ché-na
horse	pụn-nu-ká-mi-tá (elk dog)		wŭ-hok
mink	yí-kai-yi	hóħ-chev-e	
moose*	sĭk-kĭ-tŝi-sú		
mountain-goat*	a-pú-maħ-kit-ki-náw (white big horn)		
mountain-lion*	ó-maħ-ka-taí-yu (big wildcat)	na-nó-se-he-am	
mountain-sheep*	í-maħ-kit-ki-náw (big horn)	ḳós-e	
muskrat*			hí-i-ḳóħ-ťhŭ-ŭ
opossum*		ó-che-vá-se	
otter	ắm-mu-ni-si	ná-e	yé-i-yĕ
owl	sí-pĭs-to	més-ta-e	
porcupine*	kai-i-skáħp	heŝh-kó-wstŝ	hó-u-hŭ-ŭ
prairie-chicken*	kí-to-ki		
prairie-dog*	kĭ-tŝĭ-sú-maħ-ko-ka-ta	o-no-ne-vó-nesch	cha-ťhá-nĭ-i
rabbit, cottontail*	si-ká-tŝĭs-ta	he-yóv-se-tas	ná-ŭ-ḳŭ
rabbit, jack-*	ó-maħ-ká-tŝĭs-ta	aí-hnoe-vó	wa-tĭ-tă-ná-ŭ-ḳŭ (black-tipped ear rabbit)
raccoon*		matŝ-kóm	
skunk*	á-pi-kai-yi	ħá-u	ḳó-u-hŭ-ŭ
snake			sí-i-si-yĕ
spider	ksi-wa-wá-ka-si (antelope on foot)	vé-ho	ni-á-ťhaⁿ
swan*	ksĭ-kó-maħ-kai-yi		
turkey*		maħ-hé-ne	bắs-chĕn-nŭ
weasel	o-tá	ħá-e	hĭs-sé-o
wildcat*	na-taí-yu	moh-káv	bă-há-ḳăⁿ
wolf	ma-kú-yi	hó-ne	háⁿ-qi-i

CARDINAL POINTS

English	Piegan	Cheyenne	Arapaho
east	ná-moht; pi-náp-pohfš (downstream)	he-sén	ní-ith-bi-sís-sat
north	a-pát-uh-soht	no-tám	něně-bi-í-hľ i; něně-ví-hi
south	am-s-ká-poht	so-wón	na-wŭ-hŭ-ŭ
west	ním-moht; a-mí-toht (upstream)	hón-so-wón	ní-is-nǎ-í-sǎt

COLORS

black	sĭk-sĭ-ná-fši [1]	moh-tǒv	wa-ŭ-tǎ-i-ya-ŭ
blue	ófš-kui-na-fši	o-tá-tǒv	chǎ-ně-tǎ-i-ya
gray	i-ki-fší-na-fši	wóh-pa	na-ní-chǎ-ǎ-hǎ-ŭ
green	sís-ksĭm-o-qe-na-fši (new grass like)	hoh-ko-fšév	
red	iě-ku-fší-na-fši	má-a	bǎ-ǎ-ŭ
white	ksĭk-ksĭ-ná-fši	vo-kóm	nŭ-na-ŭ-chŭ-a-ŭ
yellow	oth-kú-i-na-fši	he-yóv	ni-ha-yá-ŭ-ŭ

PRIMITIVE FOODS [2]

acorns		hma-tǒ-chem	lh-ḳa-ché-ep
bitterroot	ǎ-ksĭ-ksĭ-ksi		
black-haws			sǎ-i-bí-na
buffalo-berries	mi-ksi-ní-fšim	ma-che-mé-nofš	
camas	mĭs-sĭs-á (dung)		
carrot	nis-fši-ká-pa		
choke-cherries	pák-kihp	mé-nofš	
corn		hmá-mé-nofš	há-ě-ti
currants	ó-tŭh-kui-no-ku (yellow beads)		
gooseberries	pak-sí-ni-si-man	he-stah-fšé-me-ne	
grapes		hóh-pa-fše-ná-me-nofš	
huckleberries	á-pa-waps		
partridge-berries	kák-si-yin		
pine-nuts			sǎ-ǎ-thí-bĭ-na
plums		ma-he-mé-nofš	bǎ-sĭb-i-na
prairie-turnips	mas	mo-ku-tá-énh	
prickly-pear fruit		ma-tǒ-mo-nfš	
red-osier berries	á-pi-ni-kĭm		
rose-hips	kĭn-ní-a		
service-berries	á-ku-nṳk	he-tán-e-mé-nofš	

HANDICRAFT

arrow	áps-si	mé-he	hath
arrow-point	ksĭs-sá-ko-pŭn	mó-huš	wá-a-sath

[1] Adjectives denoting color cannot be used alone. It is necessary to say, for example, "it looks black."

[2] See also under the head of Animals.

English	Piegan	Cheyenne	Arapaho
arrow-shaft	a-sĕ́ĥ-ki-man	mó-kųtš̆	ha-ná-a-chɪ-i
basket-tray		vé-no-e-toĥk	ni-ni-ắ-tha-tắ-ni-i
bow	ná-ma	mách-keo	bắ-ǎ-tǔ-ǔ
bowl, clay		ka-só-ós-che	hắ-i-ná-ǔ
bowl, wooden	mɪs-tš̆óĥ-kos	kam-ĥé-ve-tok	bĕs-ná-tǔ-i
breech-cloth	ó-kyuĥ-sa-tš̆ɪs	o-o-hmó-o-us-tš̆	
cap, skin	ɪs-tš̆ú-no-kan		chá-a-tá-ǔ^n
deerskin	ó-wa-ka-si	vŏ́-tš̆e-va-nųhtš̆	bí-hi-í-o
dress	a-sú-kas-sɪm	hó-es-tš̆	bí-i-ku-i-tá-no
hide-flesher		má-é-nu	
hide-scraper		mó-e-hna-tš̆e-to-e	
leggings	a-tš̆ɪs	mah-tó-htš̆	wa-tá-ĥa^n
moccasins	a-tš̆ɪ-kín	mo-chá-hntš̆	wá-a-hǔ-no
mortar	ɪ-tš̆ɪ-suí-pak-shɪ-nɪ-ka-map	pé-hno-e-mé-na-tš̆ [1]	
pestle	pak-shɪn-í-ki-ma-tš̆ɪs		
pipe		he-óĥ-ku	
quiver	pųn-no-pá-tš̆ɪs		
saddle	i-í-tan; kí-to-ki-o-ka-tš̆ɪs (prairie-chicken snare)		
shield	á-o-tan	ho-wáh-nu	
shirt	a-sú-kas-sɪm	és-tš̆e-e	bí-i-ku-i-tá-no
spear	sa-pa-pís-ta-tš̆ɪs	ĥó-mó-u	ka-wá-ha^n
spoon	a-pú-tš̆i		
sweat-lodge		é-ma-om	
tipi	mu-yís	vé-e	ắ^n-wu
travois	ma-nɪs-tš̆íw		
water-vessel	ksi-pǔ́-man	vé-ohtš̆	hắ-tǎ-chɪ-ná-ǔ

NATURAL PHENOMENA

ashes	máks-ki-tš̆i	pá-e	chí-i-tĥǔ-u
charcoal	sí-koks-kɪ-tš̆i	ho-ós	wá-as
cloud	so-kɪs-tš̆ɪ-kó	vó-e	hi-ná-a-ná-i-ti-i
darkness	ɪs-kí-i-natš̆ (kettle like)	é-e-a-e-no-né-to	bĕ-ní-hɪ-yá-ǔ
day	ksɪs-tš̆ɪ-kó	ésh-év	hí-si-i
earth	cháĥ-ko	hó-e	bi-i-tá-a-wǔ-ǔ
fire	ɪs-tš̆í	ho-és-ta	hɪs-sít-tǎ^n
fog	is-sí-natš̆		bắ-a-no-ú-nɪ
Great Dipper	iĥ-ki-tš̆í-kǔ-miks		
ice	kun	má-om	wá-a-wǔ
lake	ó-maĥ-sɪ-kɪ-mí	ne-hán	ní-ǎch
light	ksɪs-tš̆i-koi-na-tš̆i (day like)	e-vo-nét	na-ná-á-ǎ^n
lightning	aí-pa-pum	ho-ét	chí-hǎ^n-ǎ-ķǔt
Milky Way	ma-kú-yoĥ-so-ko (wolf road)	se-a-me-eó	bá-ha^n
mist	ắ-si-is-so-tô	ma-én-hnu	ķá-nɪ-a-sá-ǔ
moon	ko-ko-mí-kye'-sum (night sun)	ṭa-é-she	bi-ķó-u-sí-is
mountain	mis-ták	o-ho-ná	ha-há-a-ni
night	kó-ko	ṭa-e	tǎ-chắ-ǔ

[1] The Cheyenne word means both mortar and pestle.

English	Piegan	Cheyenne	Arapaho
Pleiades	mióh-pu-ku-iks (bunched)	ma-no-o-tó-cha-so	
rain	só-tô	ho-ó-ḳó	ha-sá-něch
rainbow	ná-piw-o-fŝĭ-kan; ná-piw-i-ka-tóm (Old Man he roped it)	no-no-nó	na-yát
river	ni-í-tŭh-ta	ó-he	ni-chí-a
rock	óh-ku-tuk; ó-mah-skǐm	o-ho-ná	ha-ná-ḳŭ-u
sky	spóh-tŭh-kŭ; spom-óh-tŭh-kŭ	vó-e	há-nah
smoke	si-fŝĭ	ve-no-ṭá-esh	chă-ă-ṭŭ
snow	kó-nĭs-ko	hés-to-es	hí-yĭ
star	ka-ká-to-si	ho-tó-hwch	há-tha
sun	na-tó-siw; kye'-súm	é-she	hi-sí-is
sun-dogs	o-fŝí-ik-ski-wah-sĭn		
thunder	ksĭs-fŝi-kóm	no-nó-ma-e	bá-ha-á-hŭ
water	ôh-kíu	má-pe	nǎch
wind	su-pó	há-a	hǎ-sé-i-sǎ

NUMERALS

one	tóksh-kam	nó-ka	chǎ-sě-chi
two	ná-to-kam	ní-ha	niss
three	ni-óksh-kam	ná-a	nǎ-sa
four	ni-so-ó	né-va	yenn
five	ni-si-fŝí-yi	nó-hon	ya-thán
six	ná-u	na-sóh-so-a	ní-i-ṭa; ní-i-ta-tá
seven	ih-ki-fŝí-ka	ní-soh-to-a	ní-i-sa-tah
eight	ná-ni-so-o	na-nóh-to-a	nǎ-sa-tah
nine	pih-ksó	só-oh-to-a	thí-a-tah
ten	kie-pó	ma-tóh-to-a	bǎ-tǎ-tah
eleven	ni-fŝi-kú-pu-tu	ma-tóh-to-a-óht-no-ka	chǎ-sé-i-ní-i
twelve	ná-fŝi-ku-pu-tu	ma-tóh-to-a-óht-ni-ha	nis-sí-i-ní-i
thirteen	ni-kú-pu-tu		
fourteen	ni-sí-ku-pu-tu		
fifteen	ni-si-fŝí-ku-pu-tu		
sixteen	nǎ-ku-pu-tu		
seventeen	ih-ki-fŝí-kie-ku-pu-tu		
eighteen	ná-ni-si-ku-pu-tu		
nineteen	pihk-sí-ku-pu-tu		
twenty	ná-fŝĭ-pu	ni-só-e	ni-sá-ŭ
twenty-one	ná-fŝĭ-pu-ni-fŝi-kú-pu-tu	ni-só-e-óht-no-ka	ni-sá-ŭ-chǎ-sé-hĭ-ní-i
thirty	nié-pu	na-nó-e	nǎ-sa-ŭ
forty	ni-sí-pu	ni-vó-e	ye-yá-ŭ
fifty	ni-si-fŝí-pu	no-ho-nó-e	ya-tha-yá-ŭ
hundred	kie-pí-pu	ma-toht-nó-e	bǎ-tǎ-tas-sá-ŭ

PERSONAL TERMS

aunt, maternal	see *mother*	see *mother*	see *mother*
aunt, paternal	ma-áhs (his grand-mother)	he-heá-e	hǎ-hé-i

English	Piegan	Cheyenne	Arapaho
baby	Is-sĭ-fsí-man	mé-she-hwfs	té-i-ya-ně-hí-i
boy	sah-kú-ma-pi	he-ta-né-kash-ḳon (young man)	ha-ná-ha-a-hé-hɪ
brother, elder			
vocative form	nĭ-sá		
my ——	ni's	fse-ha'-ne-hét	nă-ă-să-hă-ă
your ——	ki's	né'-ne	
his or her ——	o's	hé'-ne-heo	
brother, younger (feminine pronouns)			
vocative form	nĭ-sís		
my ——	nĭ-sís	náh-ta-ta-ném	
your ——	kɪ-sís	ne-stá-ta-ném	
her ——	oh-sís	hé-sta-ta-ném	
(masculine pronouns)			
vocative form	nĭs-kŭn-ní; fsí-ki		
my ——	nĭs-kŭn	fse-he-vá-ne-met	nă-hă-bă-hă-ă
your ——	kɪs-kŭn	és-se-ma	
his ——	os-kŭn	he-vá-sem	
chief	ní-naw		
child	po-ká-wa	kash-ḳón	té-i-ya-ně-hí-i
enemy	kah-túm	nó-fs	chah
father			
vocative form	nín-na		
my ——	nín-na	ne-heo-ó	ne-i-sá-na[n]
your ——	kín-na	é-heo	
his or her ——	ón-ně	hé-heo	
girl	a-kí-ko-wŭn	he-é-kash-ḳón (young woman)	hɪs-sé-i-hɪ-i
man	ní-naw	he-tán	hi-něn
medicine-man	na-tó-siw	na-á-e	
mother			
vocative form	na-á		
my ——	nĭ-ksís-ta	nah-ko-é	né-i-na
your ——	ki-ksís-ta	nósh-kụh	
his or her ——	o-ksís-ta	hésh-keo	
people	ma-tá-piw [1]	vós-tan-éo [1]	he-něn-ni-tă-ă-na-ŭ [1]
people (white)	ná-pi-ta-piw (Old Man people)	vé-ho	ni-á-fha[n] [2]
sister, elder			
vocative form	nĭ-sá		
my ——	nĭnsht	fsé-he-mét	nă-bi-e
your ——	kĭnsht	ném-e	
his or her ——	ụnshfs	he-mé-heo	
sister, younger	see *brother, younger*	see *brother, younger*	see *brother, younger*
uncle, paternal	see *brother, elder* or *younger*	see *brother, elder* or *younger*	see *brother, elder* or *younger*
uncle, maternal	see *brother, elder* or *younger*		
my ——		na-hán-e	nă-si
your ——		nesh	

[1] Especially Indians.

English	Piegan	Cheyenne	Arapaho
his or her ——		he-shé-heo	
woman	a-ki	hé-e	hĭs-sé-i

Trees

ash	ka-puk-síw	mo-e-tó-e	
aspen	a-shé-fsĭ-ksĭm		
birch, black	si-ku-kín-ni		
box-elder	pák-si-pais	me-s-ché-hm	
cedar	óħ-ki-ni-mim-óħ-tok (pine with odor of rose-hips)	vó-o-ve-shí-sta-tó-u	bă-ħé-i-no
choke-cherry	pa-ki-ú-nus	vín-hno-kfš	há-wa
cottonwood	ni-tá-pis-fsĭs (real wood)	ħa-ma-hóħ-fš-fš	ha-hát
elm		ho-me-nó-a	
juniper	si-ksi-no-kó-oħ-tok		
oak		hó-ko-mesh	há-wŭk
pine	pŭħ-tók	shis-ta-tó-a	hĭs-săth
willow	ma-nów; o-fsi-pís	mé-she-e-nó-e	yá-a-ḳoḳ

Miscellaneous

food	a-á-waħ-sĭn	mé-ses-tfš	bí-i-fhu-wa
forest	a-fsí-was-ku	ma-tá-a	na-yéch
large	ó-maħ-ku	ma-a-há-u	ní-hi-non
small	i-nák-u-fsiw	fš-ché-u	há-ḳŭ-chŭ-hŭ-ŭ
spirit, human	o'-tá-ki (his shadow)	mah-ta-só-hm	bă-tăn-bă-tă-ĭ-fha
spirit, ghost	stá-ô (skeleton)	mé-a-he-só-u	bí-i-te-i
spirit-land	ó-maħ-spá-fsi-ku-yi (big sand)	se-eánh	
tobacco	na-wŭk-si; ná-mĭs-fsi	ó-no-ne-eo-nó	sí-i-sá-wa

APPENDIX FOUR: Tribal Summary

Incidents of the Nez Percé War

INCIDENTS OF THE NEZ PERCÉ WAR

Chúhlĭm-maksmaks, Yellow Bull, who was born about 1830, said: "Ever since the treaty with Governor Stevens at Walla Walla, our people have been divided into two parties, each talking for itself and accusing the other of the wrong way. Lawyer's people, the Upper Nez Percés, wanted that treaty. The Wallowa people did not want it, nor did they want to have schools nor to cut their hair. After many years of much talk our people, the southern bands, were ordered to go on the reservation, but we did not do so. Then General Howard came to make us do it. We called General Howard Atĭm-kéunin [Cut-off Arm, in allusion to the loss of an arm]. He arrived at Lapwai in the spring. Joseph, Tuhulhutsút, Piópio-haihaiŭh [White Pelican], and Hushush-kéut [Head Shorn] and Álálímiatäkänin [Wind Storm], who was commonly called Looking Glass by the white people, met General Howard. He said, 'You must move to some reservation, wherever I select it.'

"Tuhulhutsút replied: 'What you have said I cannot do, because wherever Tamáluit (the creative power) has placed me to live, in that country I will live. To no other country or place will I go commanded by earthly man. From all I know, Cut-off-Arm, I wish to tell you how our people began, and how your people began. Suppose some power should plant a tree, which would be my people, and suppose the same power should plant another tree, which would be a certain distance away, and that would be your people. As these two trees grow side by side, after a while, when they become large and their branches spread out, the branches meet and interlock. Such has been our growth, and so long as these limbs cling together, we will be one people. That is all I have to say, Cut-off Arm, and it is enough to show what we believe.'

"Then General Howard replied: 'All you have said, Tuhulhutsút, I have heard, and it shows that you are a real chief. From what I heard you say, very likely you have taught me a lesson I did not understand, and at the same time, these chiefs are apt to learn a great deal from you. That is all I have to say, for it is almost noon, and to-morrow we will meet again.'

"The next morning James Reuben, a Christian Nez Percé, whose father had died on the day preceding the council, went to General Howard and said: 'My father was killed by these men, so you had better have nothing to do with Tuhulhutsút, but force them to go to the reservation.' He thought that Tuhulhutsút had killed his father by medicine-making. On the second day of the council General Howard asked Tuhulhutsút to speak first, and the chief said: 'What I said yesterday I wish to repeat. The great law has planted us separately on the earth; and when these two trees grow together, your race and mine, the branches unite between earth and sky. I shall not move to any reservation at all. I will live where I am.'

"General Howard replied: 'All you have said, Tuhulhutsút, is true. But if we should allow you to live wherever you are, you might influence these people here [at Lapwai]. They might move away. I would rather have you come into the reservation. If you do not move on the reservation, that means war between you and me. I would rather have you answer now whether you will move on the reservation.'

"Tuhulhutsút said: 'When I was first placed here before all other people, some great law placed death here also.' General Howard then commanded some soldiers to arrest Tuhulhutsút, and place him in jail. When he was locked up, General Howard asked Piópio-haihaiŭh to speak, but that chief said nothing. Then Looking Glass was asked to speak, but he would not. Hushush-kéut also was silent.

"Then Piópio-maksmaks [Yellow Pelican] was called on, and he said: 'General Howard, give me your ear and listen to me. Tuhulhutsút is already in jail, and is locked up. These Christian Nez Percés have seen me with a big drum, and with my face painted, and they did not seem to agree with that way. I want you to decide whether my dress and my use of this drum have in any way anything wrong in them.' General Howard answered: 'What you have said is true. There is nothing wrong in your ways.' He pointed to where Moscow is now, and said: 'There is a place for you to go to dig camas. There is Potlatch creek, where you can go as far as you wish. There is Oyaíp, where you can dig camas. There is a road open for you to go to the Crow country, to the Shoshoni country, and to any other place.'

"The next morning Tuhulhutsút was released, and General Howard said: 'If there is a death planted with you, so it is with me. Therefore, if you do not move into the reservation within thirty days, we shall have a war. I shall move my army to Lamáta.'

134

"About the time the thirty days were up White Bird's band was camped at Tipaħlíwam [Camas prairie], and there some young men got whiskey. One of these was Wálaitífs, whose father had been murdered by a white man. Wálaitífs rode round the camp, shooting his gun and boasting of his bravery. An old man laughed at him, and said: 'You are so brave! Why don't you go and show it by killing the man who killed your father?' Wálaitífs was my cousin. He took with him my son, Isápsís-ilpilp [Red Moccasin-top] and Hiyúmtililpkôn. When I was told of this, I rode after them and tried to get my son to come back. He said he was going with Wálaitífs, who was on his way to get his wife. Then I told him not to do anything, and I came home.[1] They went on and came to a white man's house. He was their friend. They went in, found nobody there, and took his gun. They rode on, met him, and shot him. His name was Dick. I do not know which one shot him. This was on a small creek called Tátŭtpǎ, which flows into Salmon river. From there they came toward the camp of the people. They arrived at another settler's place; he was planting. He ran, but they shot him. His name was Bob. He was a young man. Farther on they killed Henry 'Deans.' They went into his house, saw a woman, and told her, 'Stay there! All we want is what cartridges are here.' She pointed, and said, 'There may be some in that drawer.' They got the cartridges and a gun. They came out and returned home. At Slate creek they found Charley Wood, who had a store there. He said, 'This is Henry "Deans's" horse that Wálaitífs is riding.' Wálaitífs said: 'Yes, that was his horse. We have killed him.' Isápsís-ilpilp rode the other horse that belonged to 'Deans.' Wood said, 'You have killed Henry; what are you going to do with us?' He spoke in our language. Wálaitífs said: 'All those on this Slate creek we will not harm. Here we have always been treated well, and our chiefs have already made a plan that we shall fight, and that is why we have come for the guns. We will not harm your store or kill any of you. We are going home.' They came back to our camp and told us what they had done.

"They gave a gun to Big Dawn, my brother, and he rode about telling the people in a loud voice: 'This is the horse and this is the gun they have brought back! You must all remember that we have to fight now!' The three young men were then joined by Stick In The Mud, Hǎlěpkǎnut [Bare Feet], Chǎlúnin, Himniwěhěně, Pakalwainákt, Wewókiŭ-ilpilp [Red Elk], and some others, and went out to kill Mason, Sam Benedict, and others.

"When these young men were doing the killing, Joseph and Álokŭt were away hunting cattle, getting ready to move to Lapwai. Three Eagles and some others were living in the chiefs' lodges while they were absent. As soon as these young men returned from killing the white men, Two Moons went for Joseph and Álokŭt. In the meantime the camp moved to Sapáfsasħ, a place on Cottonwood creek. The only lodges left in the old camp were two single and three double ones, those occupied by Joseph, Álokŭt, Three Eagles, and others. Joseph and his brother returned from hunting their cattle, and remained there one night. Then in the morning Joseph, Álokŭt, and Three Eagles, with one other man living in the double lodge and two men occupying the single lodge, packed and went after the main party. They found that Looking Glass had gone, and that Huśhuśh-kéut had moved over above Stites on Clearwater river. They did not want to fight, so they moved away.

* * * * * * * * * * *

"The scouts near Grangeville saw the soldiers coming. Five men who had been placed on the hills to watch their movements came in one by one to report on their position. The soldiers at length were on the hill close to Lamáta, and toward evening they stopped and ate, then moved on toward us. About four in the morning they got close enough to shoot.

---

[1] Naturally Yellow Bull was not anxious to go into this part of his family history. When first telling his story of the campaign he cleverly omitted these details as to the first murders, and later, when confronted with the statement that his family were responsible for the war, he twisted and squirmed in his seat for a time, and then freely proceeded with the discussion of the affair. It was rather an interesting family group on that occasion, as the wife of Yellow Bull is the daughter of Tamáħus, the Cayuse who killed Doctor Whitman. She helped him to straighten out the historical incidents.

"In the fighting that followed, Joseph and Tuhulhutŝút fought just like any other warriors, while the active arrangement of forces was made by Ipĕlíkt-hilamkawat [Pile Of Clouds] of Hăsótoïn. The soldiers were driven back. Three Nez Percés were wounded, but none killed. Many soldiers were killed. Their guns were taken, but no scalps: their hair was short. We took ninety guns.

"We crossed Salmon river, but the people at Kămiăḣp sent word asking us to come back and protect them. These people had not taken part in the first battle. So we moved back across Salmon river, and on the way we stopped at Cottonwood creek and had a fight in which fifteen soldiers on horses were killed.

"We went on and camped at Stites, then all the people from Kămiăḣp came, and the whole party moved to Pităyíwăwiḣ, a few miles above Stites. On a hill at that place we had another fight, both parties being on the open hillside on opposite sides of a small stream. Pile Of Clouds commanded his best men to get on their horses. The soldiers were on the west, and the Indians on the east side of the creek. The mounted Indians were sent to make a flank movement around the soldiers. They started off in single file, one head-man leading them. As soon as they got about five hundred yards away, the leader was shot by the Gatling gun, and the others stopped, for they had no leader and did not know what to do. Five men on foot then began to circle round the soldiers a little farther out than the horsemen had tried it. I was one of them. We went about three hundred yards and saw the soldiers lying on the ground about one hundred yards away. Páḣatŭsh, the leader of us five, said, 'I am going to rush out and take one of them alive, and I wish you to do the same, each of you.' Just as he was about to start, a volley was fired by the soldiers, and the smoke was so thick that we could not see. Páḣatŭsh was shot in the right hand as he held his gun, and the gun was broken. He called for another gun. Nobody there could well afford to give up his gun, but Páḣatŭsh continued to call. Then he said he would go back while we others shot as fast as possible to cover his retreat. So one by one we went back, and I was the last, without any one to shoot while I ran. The Indians were pushed back and retreated to Kămiăḣp. Joseph was there, and fought like anybody else. All the Indians who had not accepted the treaty were there. We crossed the Clearwater below Kămiăḣp, and as we went up the hill we looked back and saw General Howard's army crossing. It was about the middle of the morning. They crossed where we had crossed, and about fifty young men went back to meet them, and waited in the cottonwood trees. We on the hill saw that the cavalry came first. One soldier on the other side of the river looked through field-glasses and saw Indians in the brush, and the cavalry turned back, and just then the Indians began to shoot. The distance was about four hundred yards. They shot two soldiers. Then the cannon half-way up the hill began to shoot across the river at us up on the hill. The fight lasted about half the day, until nearly sunset. We camped at Oyaíp. There occurred an encounter with Nez Percé scouts, and one of them was killed. They were with the soldiers.

"The next morning we moved on to Musselshell creek at the foot of the mountain. It was the plan of Joseph and White Bird to cross the mountains, then come back on Salmon river among the Shoshoni. Joseph was really the chief, but he appointed Pile Of Clouds as the war-leader to carry out his directions. Looking Glass, who had always been a rover and had spent much time among the Crows, insisted on going into the Crow country and getting the help of that tribe, and Joseph consented to this plan. Pile Of Clouds was a medicine-man and had visions showing the enemy: that is why he was made the leader. The enemy could not get close without his knowing it, and he often aroused the people while it was yet dark, telling them to march.

"When we got to Lolo pass two officers came to talk to Looking Glass. Then they let us go on past. After we had passed, a camp of Flatheads came to us and talked. Then after we had gone on some distance Joseph and Tuhulhutŝút planned a council and appointed the lodge of White Bird for the meeting-place. Pile Of Clouds spoke: 'Looking Glass has been leading us into the Crow country, where it is open, and we would have no chance to fight. I wish you to make me your leader again, and go back to Salmon river, where there are mountains and timber, and we can fight.' Looking Glass got up, and said: 'Be quiet! While we are going into the Crow country and away from our own, there I can talk to the great Crow chiefs and get all the help we need.' White Bird said: 'I cannot say anything about what

Looking Glass has said. If Looking Glass wants to hold the place of chief, I cannot say anything.' Joseph did not rise, but said: 'While we were fighting for our own country, there
was reason to fight, but while we are here, I would not have anything to say in favor of fighting,
for this is not my country. Since we have left our country, it matters little where we go.
Looking Glass spoke about the Crows. Very likely the Crows will join and help us. I have
nothing to say as to where we go.' Then White Bird said, 'If we go to the Crows, we must
all go.' The young men were outside saying among themselves that if they went to
Montana in the open country, the Gatling guns would kill them all.

"The next morning Pile Of Clouds rode through the camp, shouting: 'We must go to
the Crow country, and I want all to dress in their war costumes and parade round the camp.
Women, come out and see the warriors, perhaps for the last time!' After the men had
paraded round the camp several times, they came to the centre and danced. It was then
nearly evening. The next morning Pile Of Clouds rode again round the camp and ordered
the people to pack and move on, and after camp had been made again, Pile Of Clouds
ordered that the warriors should have a dance. The dance began shortly after noon and
continued the rest of the day. Other amusements were had. Young men took a rawhide
to beat on with sticks and went about the camp-circle singing a song in front of each lodge.
This was a regular custom at the large camps. On the next morning Looking Glass rode
through the camp, shouting: 'We will move to Ishkumchilâlih [Big Hole river]!' This was
only a short march. We got there before noon. There was no dancing; everybody rested.
The next morning Looking Glass rode about bidding the young men go out to see if they could
kill antelope, and the women to supply themselves with new lodge-poles. After he had gone
a short distance, White Bird rode up to him and asked him to stop and talk. He said: 'Why
is it necessary to get new poles? We are not going to the Crow country to camp. We do
not need new poles. We are trying to escape the soldiers, and there must be haste.' Looking Glass said nothing for a moment, then he rode on, continuing his orders to the men and
women. So the young men and women went out. When night came, some of the young
men proposed to go about with the rawhide, singing. About midnight they stopped singing,
and some of the boys from twelve to fifteen years of age continued to sit about the fire they
had built. A man came up on horseback with a gray blanket over his head. He came close
to the boys and looked at them, and the boys said to one another, 'He looks like a white man.'
They saw his forehead. This was a soldier, and the troops were camped two miles away.
In the morning an Indian rode across the creek for some horses, and he was fired on and shot
by the soldiers. We rushed to the fight, and tried to drive the soldiers out of their entrench-
ments up the hill. One soldier was riding round with a paper, and we thought he was keeping a count of those who were killed, but did not know whether he was counting dead Indians
or soldiers. We shot him. He rode a gray and led a black. Seventy-four of us were killed,
and thirty-three of these were men. Looking Glass was not killed here. The soldiers rushed
on foot into our camp and set fire to it, but after a while we drove them across the creek past
their ditches and into a large hole, like a mine. We watched them there all night and part
of the next day. Then Looking Glass for some reason said we would leave them, although
the soldiers had not any water. Some of our women were wounded, and we travelled slowly.

"Three days after this fight we heard that General Howard was following us with some
Shoshoni Indians, and had arrived at the place of the last battle. We moved on to the south
and met some Shoshoni. I could speak their language a little, and I went to their head-man,
who said that they would not fight. We went on and met eight large covered wagons. The
young men began to take what they wanted, and Joseph and White Bird sent me, knowing
that I did not drink whiskey, to tell them not to take whiskey. After I left, they killed some
of the drivers, and got drunk, and killed some of their own number.

"A few days later we learned from a scout that General Howard was only one day behind
us. Looking Glass rode about telling the news, and ordering everybody to prepare to meet
the soldiers. At the same time the women packed the horses and went on, and Looking Glass
filled the pipe and the chiefs smoked and discussed plans. Looking Glass wished to attack
at night. My nephew had been wounded in the previous fight, and Looking Glass came to
me and told me I had better take the young man back. So we and about sixteen others went
back from there. About a hundred and twenty proceeded to meet the soldiers, made a night
attack, and drove off a herd of mules and horses. The soldiers pursued and got some ani-

mals back, but our men brought two hundred to camp. We travelled then toward the Bannock country and camped on a big lake, where a river [the Yellowstone] runs out of it.

"In the hot springs country, before we got to the lake, some of our young men captured some white people. White Bird ordered that the people be released, for he said we were not fighting women. They were captured by some young men from Lapwai, who had joined us after the fighting began.

* * * * * * * * * * *

"After we reached the Crow country a Crow chief, son of Double Pipe, came and talked to Looking Glass, telling him that the Crows who were with the soldiers would not shoot at us with the intention of hitting us, but they would aim over our heads. Later, however, one of them shot a Nez Percé, and then we regarded them as enemies, the same as the soldiers, and knew it was useless to expect help from them. Then Looking Glass decided to try to get into the Old Woman's country. We moved down the river. Here we left an old man, whose medicine was working in him, but we had no time to make a singing, and we left him in a shelter to die. We had not gone far when, looking back, we saw a few soldiers and some Indian scouts come up to the camping place. A soldier rode round the wickiup and shot twice. We were about two miles away. Coming to a creek flowing into Elk [Yellowstone] river, we saw a large company of soldiers marching over the hill to this creek. The scouts who had shot the old man Kapáchk were following on our trail. Two days we went down the river, and that night, instead of camping early, the main party went on, while I rode back to see where the soldiers were. As soon as I formed this plan of going back, Joseph got a fresh horse and went with me. After riding back a distance each of us went about half a mile off to either side of the trail to listen. It was agreed that if we heard the soldiers we should yell and so mislead them. We saw no one. In the morning we returned and told Looking Glass we had seen no soldiers, and he said we could take our time moving.

"We came to a swift creek flowing into Elk river and camped there, and in the morning found that the Crows had run off many of our horses. Then we saw soldiers with cannon and cavalry, with Crows, Shoshoni, and the people that eat corn [Arikara]. They were in front of us. The soldiers made a charge, and the fighting lasted all day. The cavalry came round toward the front on our left, while the cannon were on our right. No Indians were killed, but I saw some soldiers fall from their horses. About sunset the soldiers began to cook their supper, and Looking Glass called us together, all the important men, one by one. He said we must go after the women and the pack-horses, and leave the young men here to watch the soldiers. So after it was dark we went on, leaving about fifty young men, who during the night captured twenty-seven horses and brought them on.

"From Elk river we went north and came to a big river [Missouri] at a place where there were some soldiers. We could cross only in that place, for there was the ford. The soldiers shot at us, and then ran. From there we went westward about ten miles, and crossed another stream and marched past the fort which was there and camped. We were hungry and some of the men went down to get food. The soldiers fired at them and then fighting began. This lasted all night. We do not know surely whether these were soldiers or not, but there were soldiers at the big river where we crossed.

"At the place we crossed the river we got plenty of food when the soldiers ran away. We went up the stream between Bear Paw mountains and the Little Rockies, and camped on a creek; but in a very little while a scout brought word that he had seen soldiers. The others believed it must have been Crows hunting buffalo. After a while we saw horses on the hills. The next morning we moved on eight or nine miles and camped again with many mountains on the left, and two peaks visible on the right. On the following day we moved only about five miles and were out from the mountains. We saw many buffalo, and killed many. We camped there. On the next morning I was out looking for my horses, but could not find them. Just about sunrise I returned and found that two men who had been in the rear to look for the enemy had come in and told the news that on the day before, just about sunrise, they had seen something far away that looked like an army, and they predicted an attack by the soldiers. Then Looking Glass said: 'Never mind what they say. Fix up your meat, so it will dry, and fix your hides so they will dry a little, and then after the sun is high we will move.' While he was saying this he turned around, then suddenly cried: 'Get your guns! Here are the soldiers!' We got our guns, but could not catch our horses. This was about eight or nine o'clock.

138

"All day we fought, and the next day, and on the third day there was a pause. A white man, George Cayuse, who spoke our language, called out: 'Have you had enough? Are you full of this fighting?' We answered, 'No, we are still hungry for war!' So the firing was resumed, and the two cannon began to shoot again. In the first day's fighting were killed Tuhulhuŧsút, a sub-chief Timīhlpúsĭmŭn [a Cœur d'Alêne name], Looking Glass, Álokŭt, and Pile Of Clouds.

"After the first day we had our caves dug, and not many were killed. About noon on the third day George Cayuse shouted that we had better stop and eat, so we ceased firing, and the women went down to the creek and got water. After dinner George Cayuse called out, trying to learn who was the chief, and we answered that Joseph was our head-chief, and White Bird the second. Then he said, 'There is no use of fighting any more.' We answered, 'Our chiefs are killed, and we may as well keep on fighting.' After a while, toward evening, Joseph decided to risk his life among the soldiers, and he called out to George Cayuse that he was coming. So he went, and Tom Hill went with him as his interpreter. The latter came back very soon, and reported that the soldiers had arrested Joseph. That evening Tom Hill left us, saying he had fought enough, and now that Joseph was prisoner he was going to leave.

"After Joseph had been gone about an hour my wife came to me and said, 'We have left a knife where we were digging the hole to fight in.' So I went with her to the place, about a hundred and fifty yards away. Just as I came to the place, we saw two men coming on horses. They had guns. I went to meet them and shook hands. One said, 'I am Captain Jerome.' He had a gun and I had none. I said, 'They have taken Joseph, and you must come with me.' So I took him back among my people. The captain led his horse to a hollow where my four horses stood out of range of bullets. He sat down in front of me, and as we sat there I heard some one in a cave behind us talking about killing him. I turned about and said: 'Our chief is over there, and what they do to him, we will do to this man. You boys, talking about shooting this captain, you had better keep quiet.' I said this as he sat there with me. They said, 'All right!' On my left was the sound of someone opening a breech-block, putting in a cartridge, closing the block, and raising the hammer. Some one came back of me and I felt a gun-barrel laid on my shoulder and pushed against my neck, and a voice said, 'Look out for your head!' I reached up and took hold of the end of the barrel, then got up, turned, and said to him: 'Our chief is over there, and if we should happen to harm this man, our chief will be killed. I want him to be left alone, so that when our chief comes back we can turn this man over.' Charley Moses could speak with the soldiers, and I told him to say to the captain that he would not be hurt. Later I said, 'I am going to leave this man here while I take his horse and go to see how Joseph is getting along.' Captain Jerome said, 'All right, I will stay here.'" [1]

Tom Hill, son of an immigrant Delaware and a Nez Percé woman, related the following:

"A white man named 'Lolly' [Larry Ott] encroached on the land of a chief at White-bird creek. The Indian remonstrated, but the white man said he had a right to it and got a gun and shot him. The wounded man lived a while, and told his friends that the white man had shot him for nothing. His son was angry and got two friends to go out and kill the white man. They killed several white people. This was the beginning of the war. In this way had the white people been treating us in those days, taking land, horses, and cattle.

"I was in the Big Hole country in Montana. We heard from some white people that the war had begun in Idaho four days before. We went northward to the Flathead country, and learned that our people were coming through the mountains by Lolo pass. We held a council and three of us started to meet our people: my brother, John Hill, another brother named Píalis, and myself. We passed down the Missoula river. We got to the fort where the soldiers were, and John Hill talked to the officer and got a note which he was to take to 'Woodbridge,' an officer who had left the fort to scout. We started out and met 'Woodbridge,' and his soldiers, among whom was a half-breed Flathead. They told us Looking Glass and

---

[1] Yellow Bull's story of the surrender and of the events following was so largely a matter of camp gossip that it hardly seemed worthy of record.

Joseph were intending to fight everybody, even their relatives. John Hill said that this was the meanest liar we could talk to. We went on and came to the hot springs — about the summit of the Bitter-root mountains — and camped, remaining there two nights. We had nothing to eat. John Hill told me to go up the road and try if I could see the people. At a big prairie I met them. I said: 'What did you come out for? It would be better for you to stay there and fight.' Looking Glass said, 'No, we must go to the Crows.' I told him, 'You are angry with all the people; you are angry even with the other Nez Percés.' He said, 'No, there is no such mind in us.' I told him what the half-breed Flathead had said. All of the chiefs declared this was not true, what he had said. They moved on and came to our camp. They asked John Hill to join them. He said: 'No! Look at my fingers; I have only two.' He had been a soldier in the big war [Civil War] and his fingers had been shot off. His father also had been through that war. So he thought it was not well for him to join them and fight the soldiers, on whose side he once had fought. They asked Píalis, and he too refused. 'I have my horses and cattle,' he said, 'and I am rich, and what will become of all these if I fight? It would have been better for you to stay there and fight.' We three then started down the creek, leaving the people at the hot springs.

"As we went — it was night — we heard ahead of us: 'Halt!' We held in our horses. 'Who's there?' we heard. 'A friend,' John Hill answered. Then from all directions they came up. An officer stood in the road, holding a gun toward us. 'Who are you?' 'John Hill.' They let us pass, and we went down to the creek and started a fire. John Hill talked to the officers, telling them of the meeting with the Nez Percés. The officers told John Hill to stay with them as interpreter, and the two of us were permitted to go. So in the morning we two went home, and John stayed as interpreter. He told us to try to stop the people from going any farther. We went home to the Flathead reservation. Not long after this I heard that John had been handcuffed and put in jail, and would be hanged. I did not believe it, and I went over to the soldiers' place [Fort Missoula] to inquire about it. A band of Nez Percés had arrived in the town, and they were buying things. We brothers had left some things in the Big Hole country, and now I went out with the people to get them and bring them home. We camped there one night, and the next night the soldiers came.

"We were surrounded. Nobody knew there was going to be a fight. Everything seemed to be quiet, and all were sleeping. I, too, was asleep. I had no moccasins or leggings on. It was about daylight, when I heard a shot. A man had put his horses across the creek, and in the early morning he was going after them. He came close to where the soldiers were, and they killed him. Then rapid firing began, while the people were yet in their blankets. Many were killed in their beds—men, women, babies. In the lodge where I was were an aunt of mine and a younger brother. The aunt was shot through the head, the brother through the loins. I cried out. I got up, without moccasins, leggings, or shirt, grasped my gun and cartridge-belt, and rushed out. The flash of the guns looked like fireworks. Three of us crossed the creek, and found there three others left of those who had already gone over. Two were killed immediately. At the upper end of the camp the soldiers set fire to some of the lodges, which were covered with cloth, some of it purchased in the stores, and some brought with the people from the Nez Percé country. The fight did not continue long before we began to drive the soldiers back. There was a little hollow, into which the soldiers went. I said, 'Let us stop!' I heard some soldiers in that hole crying. We went back to our camp, and I saw everywhere people lying dead and wounded. One woman had her head split almost in twain. It was near noon. The camp was so close to the hollow that we did not have to remain away to watch the soldiers. Not long after this it was decided, without any particular man planning it, to make another attack. We divided into two parties, and came at them from both sides. There Páhatúsh, a great warrior, known among all the Indians east of the mountains, was killed. This discouraged the others, and the fighting stopped again. His body lay close to the hole, and we decided to leave it there. We moved forward the next morning.

"Many were wounded. We did not remain there and kill the soldiers because we did not like their way of fighting in the night. It is good for the Indians to fight in broad daylight and act like men, but that way of coming up in the night we did not like, and so we did not stay there to fight.

"We went up Ross fork and met seven covered wagons. The reckless young men began to take away the goods and the horses, and I tried to make them stop. They found some whiskey and began to drink, and they set fire to the wagons. I do not know whether they killed any one. They came back and made much noise. Red Elk, one of them, came and slapped me in the face, crying: 'Why are you helping the white people? They have killed our children!' One came behind us and shot a man through the back. I was angry. I got my gun and shot Red Elk through the hand. Then all the drunken men ran away. I took the wounded man with me. We travelled on and camped.

"We heard that the soldiers were close behind, and Looking Glass told me to take charge of the party which was to go back against them. 'These are all your young men,' he said. 'Whatever you think best, take them and do it.' I told the young men to get ready, and we would go and meet them at night. When we came to their camp we crossed the creek just below them. Three good men placed themselves behind me. The soldiers were building a fire. I said: 'It is a bad thing to shoot any one while he is not ready and sleeping. It is always better while both sides are awake. We must take their horses.' Many of us had only one horse each. I told them, 'If they shoot at us, fight.' Most of the men crossed to the other side, while I remained where I was. We began to yell. Looking Glass got off near the tents, and took a horse that was tethered there. He heard some Indians talk, and thought there must be some Nez Percés among the soldiers. We drove off the mules. After we had started, we heard the bugle call, and soon saw the soldiers coming. They dismounted, and we fought. We heard that a Nez Percé had been captured by our men. He had short hair. Somebody was crying, 'Shoot him!' I told them to stop. I recognized the man; his name was George. He was crying, and he shook hands with me. He told us that Captain John and Wilson were with the soldiers. General Howard was their chief. By leading this party I became a chief.

* * * * * * * * * * *

"We came to the Missouri river at Cow Island. There was a fort at that place. I advised that we leave the people there in peace. Some of the young men were still reckless. It was daytime. I and the others were trying to keep the young men quiet. We crossed the river in the afternoon, passed round the fort, and camped about two miles away. From there some young men went back and burned the store.

* * * * * * * * * * *

"We got to our last camp. It was about nine o'clock when the soldiers charged on us. I had a wife whom I loved more than anything else. I took a horse and tied her to it, and told her to go fast. The soldiers were on all sides of us, and many of our people were soon killed or wounded. At sunset we stopped fighting. I do not remember the days very well.

"I told Joseph, White Bird, and others that I was going over to the soldiers. When I reached their lines a man on horseback, with soldiers, met me and shook hands with me. I recognized some men as Cheyenne and I shook hands with them. The soldiers told me that the chief was General Miles, and asked if I wanted to see him. I said I did. One of them got off and told me to mount his horse, and he walked at my side. He said his name was Lieutenant Jerome. After we crossed a small creek I saw the soldiers standing in line. General Miles stood there with his feet apart, and his hands on his hips. I went to him and the soldier told him I wanted to see him. He told me to get off. I did so. He shook hands with me, and said: 'You need not be frightened; nobody will hurt you. I am the chief man here. All these soldiers are my men. Are you hungry?' I said, 'Yes, I have not had anything to eat or drink.' He ordered the soldiers to go away, and we went in to eat. He sat on my right. He took out a paper, and asked me where Wálaitíłs was. I told him he had been killed at the Big Hole. 'Where is Isápsís-ilpilp?' 'Killed at the Big Hole.' 'Where is Tipialắnă-kắpskắps?' I told him that he had been killed by the Assiniboin on the second day of the fighting.[1] He had been with those who ran away. Then General Miles inquired

---

[1] The informant was in error as to Tipialắnă-kắpskắps, who is still alive. He had likely escaped from the camp, hence it was reasonable to assume that he had been killed.

about Tuhulhutsút, and I said, 'You have killed him.' 'Where is Joseph?' 'Joseph is alive over there.' 'Where is Álokŭt?' 'You have killed him.' 'Where is Looking Glass?' 'You have killed him.' 'Where is White Bird?' 'He is alive and is over there.' Those were all he asked me about. Our food was now ready. General Miles said, 'Look at all these soldiers you have killed.' I looked and saw many covered up. He smiled, and said, 'You need not be afraid.' I then ate.

"He said: 'The war is over. Call Joseph to come.' I called over to Joseph to come and bring his gun with him. General Miles was standing beside me when I called. Joseph came and I told General Miles this was Joseph. Four men came with him: Haiyaitámun, Wĕptĕsh-wăhaiŭht, Kálôwit, and Páhwéma. Miles told Joseph the war was over, and all the guns must be given up. Joseph said, 'I can give up only half of the guns; I must keep half for myself.' Miles said he must have all of them. Then he went on: 'Whatever place you select to go to, there I will return the guns to you, and the horses, and the Government will help you to live.' He told Joseph to go over to the camp and tell them to come, all of them, and to bring their guns. Then Joseph and the other four started to the camp, but Miles told me to remain. They had gone only about twenty-five yards, when Miles told me to call Joseph back. When the chief came back, the General sent me over to the camp and kept Joseph. So I went back. I came to where the Indians were and told the head-men that Joseph was left behind, and that the war was over. They paid no attention. I saw the same Lieutenant Jerome coming to us on a brown horse. When he was about half-way to us he was met by Tsĕpĕ'kikt. Then Yellow Bull stepped out and walked to Tsĕpĕk'ikt and Jerome. Tsĕpĕk'ikt had his hands on the reins of Jerome's horse, and the lieutenant got off, while the Indian took charge of the horse. Soon after that I heard that the Indians intended to kill the lieutenant. Háhats-haihaiŭh [White Grizzly-bear] and Tukălikshímă, a brother of Looking Glass, ordered me to go and see about this. I found the lieutenant sitting surrounded by the Indians. I took him away to a hollow place. Kulkul-shníni said: 'There is no reason for you to keep that man from being killed.' I replied: 'Joseph is left over there.'

"That night firing began on the soldiers' side. It did not last long. About nine the next morning we took the lieutenant to a hill and from there called out, 'Where is Joseph?' They brought Joseph out and showed him. I shouted, 'We must trade our men!' They brought Joseph about half-way, and the lieutenant went to meet him. When Joseph got back, he told us to go to our caves, we were going to fight. He said that he had been handcuffed. I gave out the word that we must face and fight, and not go into our caves. I took my gun and made ready. Two men came behind me. After going a short distance I told them to turn back, the soldiers were so many we three could not do anything. I made up my mind to tell the people to quit fighting. I was tired, and did not care what they would do to us. The women and children would be left alive anyway. Part of the Indians said, 'No, we will fight.' Others agreed not to fight. Then I said again, 'We must not fight.' I heard some-body calling; it was Captain John and George Miapkáwĭt, scouts. They had a white flag. Captain John said, 'Children, I have arrived.' I saw that one man was ready to kill these two men, and another was trying to take the gun away from him. I called out, 'We must quit fighting!' I went to meet these two men alone and shook hands with them. Some others then came and shook hands with them. Captain John, while there among us telling the news, said that he had a word from General Howard. He said we need not be afraid. I said: 'Tell me the truth, and no lies. Some have already consented to quit fighting.' Joseph called to me to go over with him; he said: 'That is the best thing we can do. You have already heard what General Miles said, that he is the head of the army, and will not do anything to us.' So all the people started over to the soldiers. White Bird and some others had gone away the night before. When we got to General Howard, I told him: 'See these people I have brought. There may be some that have not come. It may be their intention to remain away.' Chapman was interpreter for General Howard. We gave up our guns."

ILLUSTRATIONS

JOSEPH-NEZ PERCÉ

Mescal Bakers - Apache

FASTING

PIEGAN WAR-BONNET AND COUP-STICK

LITTLE DOG – BRULÉ

A Piegan Play Tipi

Potter Building Her Kiln

THE GRIZZLY-BEAR—PIEGAN

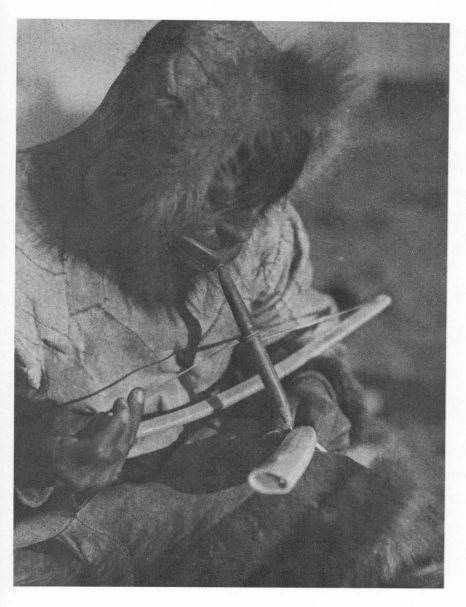

Drilling Ivory, King Island

TÓNENÍLÍ, TOBADZÍSCHÍNÍ, NAYÉNĚZGANÍ - NAVAHO

ARAPAHO MAIDEN

RETURN OF SCOUTS—CHEYENNE

PIEGAN CAMP